What readers say about Harlequin Romances

"Your books are the best I have ever found."
P.B.*, Bellevue, Washington

"I enjoy them more and more
with each passing year."
J.L., Spurlockville, West Virginia

"No matter how full and happy life might be,
it is an enchantment to sit
and read your novels."
D.K., Willowdale, Ontario

"I firmly believe that Harlequin Romances
are perfect for anyone who wants to read
a good romance."
C.R., Akron, Ohio

*Names available on request

OTHER
Harlequin Romances
by ELIZABETH ASHTON

Voyage of Enchantment

by

ELIZABETH ASHTON

Harlequin Books

TORONTO • LONDON • NEW YORK • AMSTERDAM • SYDNEY

Original hardcover edition published in 1977
by Mills & Boon Limited

ISBN 0-373-02093-7

Harlequin edition published August 1977

Printed in U.S.A.

CHAPTER ONE

'OH, Uncle Matt, how absolutely marvellous!' Audrey
Winter exclaimed ecstatically. 'But why should you? I
mean you ... you've never taken much notice of me before.'

'That was my omission.' The middle-aged man behind
his imposing desk smiled with gratification at her enthusiasm. 'After all, you're my goddaughter, and I've
never done anything for you before beyond the silver
mug I gave you at your christening. I'm afraid I'm not
very good with children, never having had much to do
with them. They seem to me to belong to a woman's
sphere when they're young, while the man of the house
is fully occupied with the upkeep of the home.'

Being devoted to her father, Audrey could not agree
with this view, but being in awe of Matthew Gregory
she did not voice her disapproval. He seemed to have
forgotten her presence and was doodling on the pad before him with a brooding look upon his heavy face. He
was not really her uncle, but being a close friend of Mr
Winter's he had been a familiar figure in her home
throughout her childhood, though he never gave her
more than an absent-minded pat on the head, and a
casual 'How are you, child', without waiting for a reply.
Her mother would whisk her away, saying that Uncle
Matt wanted to talk to her father, a proceeding Audrey
resented, especially if Matthew's visit coincided with the
hour after tea which her father always devoted to her.
Her mother explained that their guest was lonely, and
needed her father's company. He had said theirs was the
only house that felt like home to him.

When she was older, Audrey discovered that Matthew had been married, but it hadn't worked out. Hermione was Greek and had gone back to her own people taking their infant son with her, declaring that she did not want him to be brought up a hybrid; a cruel thing to say, for Matthew, though half Greek himself, claimed British nationality and was proud of it. Not that Matthew ever mentioned Hermione or his son in her hearing. Since the break-up of his marriage, which had occurred before Audrey was born, he had absorbed himself in his business.

Recalling her presence, Matthew ceased to doodle and gave a sharp sigh. He shot her a keen penetrating glance across the intervening desk top. He had a forceful personality and she was not wholly at ease with him.

'Now your childhood is behind you and you've developed into a very charming young woman, it's only right that you should be given an opportunity.'

She wrinkled her fine dark brows at this odd way of describing his munificence.

'Opportunity, Uncle Matt?'

'Of seeing something of the world,' he said suavely, and she relaxed. For a second she had sensed some ulterior motive behind his offer of a holiday cruise, which was quite absurd.

'I'll love that,' she declared fervently, and he smiled a little wryly.

'I hoped you'd be pleased.'

Matthew Gregory was of middle height and increasing girth. He might in his youth have been handsome, but now his forceful face was heavily scored with lines and wrinkles and his hair had receded. Only the eyes under his heavy brows were still remarkable, large dark eyes, from his Greek heritage, that were somehow Oriental. They seemed to hold all knowledge of the wickedness of the world of which he had grown weary, and by all ac-

6

counts he had lived life to the full.

Audrey worked in the City, and she had received a telephone message to visit him this lunchtime with some trepidation. She could not imagine what he wanted to see her about. She had never been alone with him before, apart from her parents. The offer he had made astonished her; she could hardly believe he really meant it.

'Had you made arrangements for your holiday?' he asked her. 'If so they must of course be cancelled.'

Then she recollected that she was not free unless she ditched Cheryl, and that she could not possibly do. With a little sigh she told him:

'I don't think I can. I'd arranged to go camping with a friend in the Lake District ...'

He interrupted with a shocked expression. 'Camping! Good God!'.

'Accommodation is so expensive,' she began, taken aback by his vehemence.

'And you mean to say your father has allowed it? Anything might happen to you.'

'Oh, we'll be all right. It's a big camp, there'll be lots of others.'

'Hippie types, I suppose.' His lips curled in a sneer.

'Not at all!' She was indignant. 'We're all perfectly respectable.'

Actually she did not know what her fellow-campers would be like. Her friend Cheryl Grant had done all the organising, lured by the prospect of a horde of brawny young men whom she hoped would be accessible. It had been a gesture of independence upon Audrey's part. Hitherto she had been content to go away with her parents, usually to stay with her mother's people who had a farm where she had learned to ride, play tennis with the neighbours and go to agricultural shows. Cheryl had derided such pastoral pursuits and come up with the camping notion: Audrey, turned twenty, should strike

7

out on her own. Parents, however dear, could be a brake upon holiday amusements, and this vacation in the Lake District would be an adventure with all sorts of possibilities.

Regretfully she told him: 'It's most awfully good of you, Uncle Matt, but we've made all our arrangements and I can't let my friend down.'

'Your friend?' He frowned. 'A young man?'

'Oh no, a girl from the office where I work.'

Was it relief she glimpsed in his eyes? She couldn't be sure.

'You can cancel these absurd arrangements and you can take your friend with you. In fact it's a good idea. You can share a cabin.'

'But . . .'

He grinned. 'That's a word I dislike. What's the objection? Won't she leap at the chance of a holiday afloat?'

'Yes, but . . .' He frowned at the repetition of the word. 'I mean, I don't see how. Daddy said the *Andromeda* was booked solid for the next twelve months.'

Mr Winter was the manager of a travel agency and had had his share of Sea-Air's bookings for the new ship that was making her maiden voyages that summer. Audrey knew that cruise vessels were among Matthew Gregory's many investments, but he couldn't know how popular the *Andromeda* was. She had been tremendously advertised, and many people had made reservations for more than six months ahead.

'What do you take me for?' Matthew growled. 'Do you think I'd offer you something that wasn't available?' He grinned mischievously. 'There are some advantages in being a part-owner.' She stared at him in surprise and his grin widened. 'She belongs to a Greek line and I have many shares in it. Sea-Air have chartered her, but I insisted that several cabins be reserved for my friends, in

8

case I needed them. So you take your friend along and have a bumper time.'

'It'll be wonderful. Have you told Daddy?'

'Of course, but I said I wanted to tell you myself and ... er ... see how you took it.'

And how I looked, Audrey supplemented silently. She had a suspicion that if he had been disappointed in her appearance he would not have persisted with his offer. Her prior arrangements would have given him an excuse to back out. She ought to be wildly elated; though her father might at some time have managed a modest cruise for his family, had in fact suggested it as a future possibility, the *Andromeda* was beyond his purse even with a discount, but there was something in Matthew's manner which caused her a vague uneasiness. He was regarding her with intent appraisal, as if he were summing her up for some subtle purpose that she could not divine.

At first glance Audrey Winter did not strike the beholder as anything outstanding, only upon closer examination did her good points become apparent. Her pale fine hair was an affliction to her, it was so soft and straight that it was impossible to manipulate. She had wanted, at Cheryl's instigation, to have it cut and waved, but her parents' dismay had deterred her. She wore it plaited in a door-knob in the nape of her neck, the only way in which she could keep it tidy for work. This style did show the beautiful modelling of her head and neck, and the exquisite line of her jaw. Her features were regular and her eyes were lovely, wide spaced and a clear grey, dark-lashed beneath level brows. A connoisseur in female looks would have seen the latent beauty in her face, less discerning people merely dismissed her as nice-looking. Matthew had discernment, and his sly glance slid over her slender, still slightly immature figure and rested upon her long legs sheathed in silken tights. He could

9

find no fault with those, but for his taste she was too thin, he admired more opulent curves, but the girl had an air of refinement that pleased him and no doubt she would fill out as she grew older.

She fidgeted under his close scrutiny, which she began to find embarrassing. Finally she exclaimed pertly:

'You *have* seen me before, you know!'

He smiled wryly. 'I still thought of you as an ungainly schoolgirl, not a species to be honest to which I'm partial, but now I see you've blossomed. How old are you, my dear?'

'Oh, Uncle Matt, don't you remember?' she reproached him. 'And you my godfather, as you've just mentioned. I'm coming up to twenty-one.'

'Of course you must be—how the years fly by! Twenty-one—h'm. Have you ... er ... a boy-friend, as I think you call them nowadays?'

He put the question negligently, but his keen gaze suggested that her answer was important to him.

'No one special,' she replied before it occurred to her that it was none of his business. What was her love life to do with him?

But it was quite true that she had formed no permanent connection and had not thought much about marriage; she was too happy and contented with her home and her work. Naturally there had been episodes, but her experiments hadn't gone beyond a little mild petting. She had an antipathy to physical contact with other people and she had not met a man who did not faintly repel her when he became amorous. 'Miss Touch-me-Not,' she was teased at the office, and 'the Vestal Virgin' at the parties to which she was occasionally persuaded to go. The appellation was more appropriate than they knew, for Audrey was passionately interested in antiquity and ancient history, a trait that had been encouraged by her father, who was something of an amateur archaeologist in his spare time. So also was Matthew Gregory, and it was a mutual hobby that had drawn them together.

Matthew gave what appeared to be a sigh of satisfaction.

'I hope you're not permissive?' He inquired.

'Good heavens, no!' She was shocked. 'Really, Uncle Matt!'

He laughed. 'I apologise, your father's daughter couldn't be other than a good girl and I know you've been well brought up.'

Audrey did not appreciate this gratuitous testimonial at all. Though she was a thoroughly nice girl and she had been well brought up, she yearned to be thought modern and sophisticated, but she did not know how to set about emancipating herself, for she loved her parents and did not want to upset them, though she recognised that they were inclined to be over-protective because she was their only child. Goodness implied dullness and priggishness. Her friend Cheryl's great attraction for her was that she was much less inhibited. She said and did daring things and Audrey sought to imitate her, but only succeeded in embarrassing herself, for Cheryl's main interest in life was the opposite sex. Audrey's natural fastidiousness shrank from her friend's blatant approach in that direction, and though Cheryl laughed at her, she always retreated when her timid advances met with reciprocal overtures.

Not wishing to appear naïve to Matthew, she said provocatively:

'I've had my moments.' Honesty compelled her to add, 'But somehow they never came to anything.'

'I'm glad of that,' he declared emphatically. Catching her inquiring glance, he went on: 'Forgive my inquisitiveness, but I'm half Greek and I believe like Solomon that the price of a virtuous woman is above rubies.'

Yet he was separated from his wife and he did not

11

look as if he had lived like a monk.

'What about the *hetaerae*?' she asked, showing off her knowledge. 'Weren't they admired?'

The *hetaerae*, as he would know, were the ancient Greek courtesans, cultivated women and companions of their country's most famous men.

'Ah, but they were exceptional.' He looked at her a little sadly. 'Exceptions are rarely happy. Believe me, for the normal woman, marriage and children are her most satisfactory destiny.'

Audrey nearly said how Victorian, but checked herself. Women's Lib would have something to say to Mr Matthew Gregory and Cheryl would scorn his views, but he had just offered her a superb holiday and she did not want to antagonise him, so she merely nodded her head noncommittally.

He proceeded to outline the details of her trip and enquired her friend's name. The tickets would be sent to her within a few days, and they would need to obtain passports if they had not already got them. The cruise date was only a month away; it coincided with their holiday, which would indicate that he must have checked with her father. Finally he took out his cheque book and wrote out a cheque.

'You'll need some smart clothes and evening dresses,' he remarked, handing it to her. 'Get yourself something suitable with this.' He glanced at her critically not liking the plain skirt and blouse she wore, her office outfit. 'Something glamorous.'

The amount staggered her. 'Uncle Matt, I can't accept ...'

He stopped her with an arrogant gesture.

'You must do me credit. It may be discovered you're connected with me.'

'But ...'

'Didn't I tell you I dislike that word? Take it, Audrey.

12

I've always forgotten your birthdays, so accept it in lieu of all the presents I should have given you.'

'I don't know why you're being so generous to me,' she cried.

A curious look came into his eyes; he seemed about to say something, then changed his mind. There was a short tense pause, while she nervously folded the cheque and put it into her handbag, then he said gruffly:

'Is there any reason why a lonely old man shouldn't give an old friend's daughter a bit of pleasure? And you're my godchild. I've done precious little for you up till now.'

She was certain that he was covering up what had been in his mind, and wondered uneasily if there were some ulterior motive behind his largesse, but she dismissed her suspicion as unjustifiable as soon as she left his office. It was as he said, a kind gesture, and she knew he was wealthy enough to be able to indulge in such whims. She waited impatiently for the afternoon to go by so that she could acquaint Cheryl with the good fortune that had befallen them. She was being given a marvellous present and to imagine obscure motives behind it was looking a gift horse in the mouth, a proceeding she had been taught was reprehensible. Opportunity had knocked and now she could spread her wings untrammelled by parental supervision, and under Cheryl's guidance embark upon an adventure of limitless possibilities. In short, they would have fun!

During the days that followed Audrey was too excited to be disturbed by the faint misgiving that had stirred in her during Matthew's interrogation. Cheryl of course had no qualms. If an eccentric old gentleman wished to benefit them, why ask questions? They should rejoice in their good luck. Audrey shared the lavish cheque Matthew had given her with Cheryl, for she felt she could not go expensively clad while her friend had to scrimp, and Cheryl had no scruples about accepting her gift. They enjoyed an orgy of spending, buying evening dresses, swim-wear and light dresses for going ashore. Mr Winter warned them that some countries took exception to shorts or even trousers, and they had no wish to give offence. He had been delighted by Audrey's news, and remarked that since the old boy was rolling, it was about time he did something for his goddaughter.

'Which is a relationship taken much more seriously in Greece than it is here,' he told her. 'In that country god-parents are often of more account than real parents, and expect to have a large say in the marriage arrangements.'

'Well, neither Uncle Matt nor anyone else is going to interfere with mine if ever I decide to get married,' Audrey declared firmly, remembering how Matthew had questioned her about her boy-friends. Surely he would not presume to dictate to her upon such an important issue? Besides, of what possible interest could her matri-monial prospects be to him?

'No, of course not,' her father said hastily, 'he knows English girls choose their own mates.'

He exchanged a glance with his wife, which Audrey intercepted. She looked from one to the other.

'Look, are you and Uncle Matt hatching some sort of plot between you?' she demanded.

'Plot?' Arthur Winter's air of bewildered innocence was almost too well assumed to be genuine. 'My dear child, what absurd fancy is this? Your mother and I are merely overjoyed that Matt is going to give you such a splendid holiday, which you richly deserve. I've always told him what a satisfactory daughter you are.'

'He said he'd told you about it.'

'He did mention it, but I didn't say anything to you in case he changed his mind,' Arthur admitted. 'But I didn't know it was to be the *Andromeda*. She's a new vessel and

14

maybe he wants to have your report on her when you return.'

That didn't seem very likely to Audrey, for surely he would have access to more expert opinions than hers. Her father had turned, almost it seemed to her with relief, to a pile of brochures—there were always brochures littering the Winters' home—and picked one up.

'Let's check on her itinerary, or have you already done so?'

'No, I was going to ask you about it.'

Arthur referred to the gaily coloured sheets. 'She's a Greek ship and all her personnel are Greek, though Sea-Air have chartered her.' Arthur Winter was an agent for Sea-Air. 'But you knew that. There will of course be Sea-Air representatives aboard to handle the excursions. Istanbul is her farthest port of call, and she'll visit Crete and Athens. Athens is the cradle of western civilisation—you must be sure to see the Acropolis.'

'I might prefer a night club,' Audrey said mischievously, well knowing that Cheryl would. 'I'm told the night life of Athens is quite something.'

'You wouldn't be a daughter of mine if you did,' Arthur returned confidently, and there he was right. Audrey would much prefer ancient ruins to night clubs.

The tickets duly arrived and the girls' excitement mounted. Audrey did not see Matthew again, though she wrote to thank him on behalf of herself and her friend. He had gone abroad somewhere, her father informed her, but her letter would be given to him on his return.

'And of course he'll want to see you when you come back,' he told her, 'to hear all about it.'

Audrey assented; she had no premonition then of in what strange circumstances she would next meet Matthew Gregory.

They were to fly out to Venice to join the ship. Audrey

15

had never flown before, but Cheryl had. She had once spent a holiday in Austria and talked like a seasoned traveller. A little older than Audrey, she had a certain style, though she was not pretty; a thin dark girl, she possessed a malicious wit that Audrey found amusing, though she did not believe in Cheryl's sulphurous stories of her amorous adventures, which she was fond of relating. Being inclined to be shy and diffident Audrey had come to rely upon Cheryl's support when they went out together.

At last the great day came, and they set out for the airport. To Audrey the whole procedure of air travel was thrilling and novel—the weighing of her luggage, going through passport control, the wait in the departure lounge while planes rose and descended on the tarmac outside—and she found Cheryl's bored indifference trying.

'You needn't let everyone know you haven't flown before,' she said irritably, noticing Audrey's wide-eyed wonder.

'Why not? It's true,' her friend inquired.

'Makes you seem such a wet,' Cheryl declared repressively.

'I don't care, and nobody here is interested in my reactions,' Audrey pointed out, indicating the seething crowds, which were too intent upon their own business to notice two insignificant girls.

As it was a hot day, she wore a thin dress printed in gay colours, sweet pea shades, blue, mauve and pink, with white sandals and her hair loose upon her shoulders. Cheryl, in scarlet trousers and a white top, said that she looked old-fashioned and dowdy and why on earth didn't she get her hair cut, which considerably deflated her. She did not realise that the other girl was jealous because she was attracting far more masculine glances than she did, something of which she was quite unaware. Seeing

16

her drooping lips, Cheryl relented and declared she was being catty and Audrey looked fresh and charming as a picture, so what, which as Audrey wanted to appear sophisticated did not do much to comfort her.

She did not enjoy her first flight because the aircraft was close-packed, which gave her a faint feeling of claustrophobia. The palpitating moment when the machine rose in the air was fraught with apprehension, which soon passed when the moment came to unfasten her belt and they were cruising smoothly along with the country a chequered map below them. She had read so many accounts of aeroplane flights and now she was actually experiencing the real thing. A meal was brought to them neatly packed into its tray, with little envelopes of powdered milk and sugar for the tea or coffee poured into plastic cups. Actually it was breakfast, and though they had made an early start, Audrey was too excited to do more than nibble at a roll. Cheryl ate her portion of bacon and sausage as well as her own, remarking that it was a pity to waste it. Though she was so thin she always displayed a good appetite.

The plane crossed the Alps, the grey and white mountains discernible far below, for it was a clear day. Audrey peered at them eagerly, vowing that some day she would visit them. Then followed a confusion of purple, brown and green, the Italian lakes, and finally the flat plain surrounding Venice. Italian officials gave them a casual glance as they went through to the waiting coaches presenting their passports. Audrey had not realised that Venice was an island connected to the mainland by a two-mile causeway over which the traffic raced alongside the railway, and that both were halted on the further side, not being permitted to enter the town, which was mainly waterways. Berthed a short distance from the causeway was the *Andromeda*, a white palace of a ship

17

which was to be their home for the next fourteen days.

Their cabin was nicely appointed, with its own bathroom and a square of window over the dressing table between the two beds. Looking at the window with surprise, Audrey remarked that she had expected a porthole.

'They have those on the lower decks,' Cheryl informed her, 'didn't you notice while we were waiting to embark? I see our luggage has been fetched up.' She pointed to their cases. 'This is quite luxurious, Audrey, your sugar-daddy has done us proud.'

'Oh, don't be absurd,' Audrey laughed. 'Uncle Matt's my godfather, and sugar-daddies went out with the twenties along with cloche hats.'

'Some godfather!' Cheryl grinned. 'I wish I had an uncle like that.'

But Matthew Gregory wasn't her uncle, and he was a shrewd, devious businessman who rarely did anything without a reason, nor was he famed for philanthropy. Audrey was again conscious of a faint stir of uneasiness which she instantly quelled. Matthew was far away and they were actually on board the *Andromeda*, nothing could alter that. Nor could she imagine that he would demand any sort of recompense for his generosity. It was as he had said, he was an ageing man who wanted to give his old friend's daughter a good time.

The *Andromeda* sailed during the afternoon. After exploring the several lounges and the general layout of the ship, besides booking second sitting for lunch and dinner, the two girls sat on deck watching Venice pass by as the *Andromeda* followed her pilot down the Canale della Giudecca into which the Grand Canal flowed when it reached the Palace of the Doges. A commentary over the tannoy informed them of what they were seeing. Behind the palace were the domes of San Marco, looking, Cheryl said, like dirty mushrooms. They could see the

18

crowds in the Piazza San Marco and discern the Bridge of Sighs. The sea was the greeny-blue of Canaletto's paintings, and the red roofs, campaniles and church domes slid by like the reels of a travel film. The Lido di Jésolo was to starboard, the disembodied voice told them, and Audrey giggled. 'I'll never remember if that's left or right,' she said.

The *Andromeda*'s siren sounded, making them jump, as a fleet of small sailing boats crossed her bows with the same rash impetuosity that Italian drivers showed on the roads.

Cheryl's attention wandered from the scenery to the other passengers, a large proportion of which, to her disgust, appeared to be middle-aged. But there was a fair sprinkling of young men and girls whom she eyed speculatively. Audrey knew from her expression that she was looking for likely prey. She herself was too thrilled and happy to bother about possible men friends.

A slim young waiter in white jacket and black trousers appeared expertly balancing a tray of drinks; he was dark and Greek and Cheryl watched him speculatively.

'The staff is much better-looking than the passengers,' she murmured regretfully. 'Do you suppose they fraternise?'

Shouldn't think so,' Audrey returned indifferently.

Suddenly Cheryl sat bolt upright and clutched her arm. 'I say, what about that?'

Startled, Audrey turned in the direction of her gaze.

He wasn't one of the staff, as his fawn trousers and knitted shirt proclaimed. He was standing at a little distance and appeared to be observing them though dark glasses obscured his eyes. Audrey thought he must also be Greek, for his classic face and crisp black hair did not look English or American, though he could be Latin. Tall, but not excessively so, he carried his lean muscular body with an arrogant grace. With her mind running on ancient Greek perfection of form, Audrey murmured:

'Adonis.'

She pronounced it in the Greek manner, À-thoni, and not recognising the name, Cheryl demanded:

'Do you mean you know him?'

'Oh no, merely that he puts me in mind of a classical prototype.'

'You and your classics!' Cheryl jeered. 'But whoever he is, he's watching us.' She began to preen herself, throwing provocative glances towards the object of their interest.

'You can't be sure with those sun-glasses,' Audrey objected.

Cheryl giggled. 'I can always detect admiration.'

She started to struggle up from her low seat, then sank back again with an expression of disgust.

'I'm afraid we're not in the running.'

A girl had come up behind 'Adonis' and laid a possessive hand on his arm. She could only be described as lovely, with a mane of corn-coloured curls surrounding a porcelain face as yet untouched by the sun. Her willowy figure was displayed in close-fitting blue trousers and a thin tank top. The man turned to her with a devastating smile revealing even white teeth, and Cheryl sighed.

'The best ones are always booked,' she complained. 'Still, one never knows.' She brightened. 'He might like a change, and he was certainly staring at us.'

'You wouldn't want to break up their romance,' Audrey reproached her. She was puzzled because 'Adonis' reminded her of someone else, and she couldn't think who. He seemed vaguely familiar, but she was certain she had never seen him before.

'Given half a chance I'd smash it to atoms,' Cheryl declared. 'And I'll bet that fellow isn't the ever-faithful type. You watch, my innocent, you'll see more than one change of partners during the next fortnight.'

'I don't like flirtatious characters,' Audrey said disdainfully.

'Oh, you're still wet behind the ears. They're the ones who provide the fun, and no one takes holiday affairs seriously.'

The intriguing young man had strolled off with his fair companion clinging to his arm. The first sitting for dinner was announced over the tannoy and the passengers began to drift away from the deck.

It wasn't customary to change for dinner on the first night at sea, so Cheryl suggested that they should go below and finish their unpacking, which they had left to view the Venetian scene.

'I wonder what the food's like,' she remarked. 'I hope they don't give us octopus. Somehow I don't fancy it even if it is Greek.'

'I'm ready to try everything—once.' Audrey announced gaily as they made for the companionway to the lower decks, which on the *Andromeda* consisted of wide flights of carpeted stairs.

'Don't be too rash, Cheryl advised, with a glance at her friend's animated face. Excitement made Audrey look very pretty. 'Even one attempt can prove fatal with some experiences.'

'I don't mean what you mean,' Audrey objected, as they reached the long corridor that led to their cabin. You've got a one-track mind. I shan't have any affairs.'

'Famous last words,' Cheryl observed drily as she fitted their key into the lock of their cabin door.

Venice and its outlying islands vanished into the dusk astern as the lights came on all over the ship.

CHAPTER TWO

AT dinner, to Cheryl's disgust, their table companions were two elderly women. She had cherished visions of ship's officers presiding over the meal. The big restaurant was so crowded that they could only identify their nearest neighbours, and they were not prepossessing. Miss Green and Mrs Archer were sisters, the latter being a widow. Although they had only modest means they saved enough to go on a trip every other year, and these cruises were the high spots in their drab existences. Mrs Archer interpreted Cheryl's glance correctly and smiled wryly.

'I guess you're disappointed, dear,' she said frankly, 'to be put with us instead of two young men, but I'm afraid there aren't many unattached males aboard. You'll have to console yourself with the waiters.'

'I'd be hard up if I have to do that,' Cheryl sniffed.

'Oh, some of them get very matey,' Miss Green informed her. 'The women like it, but of course they're only thinking of their tips.'

Cheryl looked round the close-packed room where the waiters threaded their way expertly between the tables. Some of them were mere boys and good-looking. 'Well, if the worst comes to the worst I'll have to make do with what I can pick up,' she said darkly.

Their own attendant, who went by the grandiloquent name of Perikles, presented her with a dish of hors d'oeuvres. He had not much English. 'Loverly, loverly,' he declared, and Audrey tried not to laugh. She selected in her turn several olives, and decided they were not an experiment she would repeat.

22

Cheryl inquired when he had gone, 'Where does the Captain feed?'

'I don't know,' Mrs Archer admitted, 'but you'll meet him tomorrow night. He'll be giving a cocktail party to meet the passengers. At least that happens on all the cruises I've been on, and I don't suppose this one's any exception. Oh, I was thrilled when we managed to get reservations on the *Andromeda*. I believe this is her maiden voyage.'

Her sister said lugubriously, 'Let's hope she's luckier than the *Titanic*. She went down on her first voyage.'

'There aren't any icebergs in the Adriatic,' Mrs Archer hastened to reassure her, and Audrey said that she did not think this was the ship's maiden voyage, though it was her first season.

'We'll be having boat drill tomorrow morning,' Mrs Archer went on. 'I expect you've noticed the life-jackets in your cabin?'

'So that's what those orange bundles are on top of our wardrobe,' Audrey exclaimed with interest. Far from resenting her companions, she found them pleasant and thought their experience might be useful. She had already lost herself on the big ship with its numerous lounges and long corridors, for she was never sure if she were moving fore or aft. Unlike Cheryl, she liked female companionship.

'Breakfast is an open sitting,' Miss Green told them, 'so we shan't see you then. It's as well to be early as you might have to wait if you're late. Jane and I always have it in our cabins, you can if you don't want anything cooked.'

'Thanks, but we've already discovered that,' Cheryl said shortly, having noticed the order cards on their dressing table. Audrey had no intention of availing herself of that service. She had been introduced to the swimming pool up on the after deck and had decided her

23

day would begin with a swim before it became too crowded.

After dinner they had a drink in one of the lounges, idly taking stock of their fellow passengers. A middle-aged American asked to join them and Cheryl brightened. Soon they were exchanging personal information, inaccurate in Cheryl's case—she said she was a model. Audrey didn't undeceive him, though she hoped they wouldn't see a great deal of Beverley—which he said was his name—as she was sure to make slips. But Cheryl did not intend that she should and soon persuaded him to take her up on deck to 'see if there was a moon'. He asked Audrey to accompany them, but she caught a sour look from Cheryl and said that she was ready for bed.

It had been a long day full of new impressions and Audrey was genuinely tired. She sat alone for a little while scrutinising everyone who passed, but nowhere did she see the handsome Greek nor his beautiful companion, and became aware that she had been subconsciously watching for them. Finally she went below to her cabin.

She awoke to bright sunlight outside the window. It was early and Cheryl was still asleep; she had come down very late the night before and Audrey had not heard her come in. Softly, so as not to disturb her, Audrey got up and slipped into the bathroom. She put on her swimsuit, a white one with practically no back, and twisted up her hair under a white rubber cap. Enfolding herself in a striped wrap and taking her towel, she ran down the corridor and up the stairs to the deck.

This had just been swabbed and glistened with wet under the canvas awning. The pool itself was exposed to the sky, and surrounded by a broad-tiled rim upon which she dropped her towel, wrap and the suntan lotion she had also brought. There was no one else there except a bored steward, and congratulating herself upon her early rising she plunged into the cool green water.

The pool was not large, a couple of strong strokes took her its length, but it was refreshing. Above her the sunlight poured down out of a cloudless sky, but it was not yet too hot. Presently she came out and sat on the tiled rim, took off her cap and shook out her hair, and it fell about her shoulders like a pale amber cloud reaching past her waist. She began to rub her legs with the lotion, hoping they would soon tan. She had a thin sensitive skin and had to moderate her sunbathing.

A slight sound caused her to shake back her hair and look up. A man was standing above the ladder leading down into the pool—diving was forbidden—having come like herself for an early dip. He had acquired his sun-tan, for the lithe lean body fully exposed except for swimming trunks was a rich golden hue and smooth as marble. If he possessed body hair he had shaved it off, and he reminded her of the figures in the Greek frieze with which one of the lounges was decorated. His proudly-held head was covered with curly dark hair cut short, and she recognised him as the man they had seen upon the promenade deck on the previous day, but this morning he was alone.

Audrey was near enough to discern his features, no longer disguised by sun-glasses, and his was an arresting face, even for a member of a country where beauty among the young is commonplace, though he was not in his first youth. He had the fine features, clear skin and long-lashed eyes so frequently depicted by Greek artists portraying their saints in the Greek churches, but there was none of the melancholy weakness such faces often betrayed, and his mouth was larger and firmer than theirs. Nor was there anything saintly about his regard. The beautiful eyes held an expression which suggested he had sampled all the pleasures of the sinful world and found them lacking; in short, he looked slightly decadent.

He saw her, naturally; he couldn't fail to do so, as she was the only person at the pool. He gave her a long speculative look and then he smiled, the same charming smile she had noticed when she had seen him before, that lit his dark face like a sunbeam through clouds. Audrey was aware of a faint stir of excitement. She had never met anyone so devastating before.

'Good morning, you're about early,' he said. His voice was pleasant and resonant with no trace of accent, and she wondered if she had mistaken his nationality; but that face could only belong to Greece, Apollo and Adonis rolled into one. 'It's the best time for a dip,' he went on. Later ...' he shrugged his shoulders expressively.

'That's what I thought,' she agreed, 'and it's going to be very hot.'

Banal words, but his dark eyes were more expressive than his speech. His handsome mouth was marred by a slightly sardonic twist and he was studying her every feature appraisingly. She could not hope it was with admiration, and she feared he was comparing her unfavourably with the lovely woman he had been accompanying when she had first seen him.

She found his intent gaze disconcerting and shook her hair forward over her face, aware that she had blushed, and became apparently absorbed in massaging the oil into her legs, though actually she was painfully conscious of him.

'Don't let me keep you from your swim,' she murmured.

'It's hardly that in such a duckpond,' he said, laughing. 'I didn't expect to meet Psyche new risen from her bath.'

'Psyche?'

26

'There's a picture by Lord Leighton that I once saw, of which you remind me. It's no doubt despised as Victorian now, though she looks very charming. All rosy-tinted flesh, but I suppose you want to acquire the fashionable sun-tan?'

'Of course. I feel a bit naked without it.' She blushed again at her ill-chosen words. Wasn't that just what he had been implying? She reached for her towelling wrap and enveloped herself in it.

'That's too bad,' he complained. 'Don't you like being admired?'

'I'm nothing to write home about,' she said hastily, embarrassed by the glint in his eyes, 'and you've acquired the best-looking female on the boat.'

'I don't follow you.'

'I saw you yesterday with that gorgeous blonde.'

His eyelids flickered. 'You saw me with Daphne? Yes, she is rather gorgeous,' he sounded bored. 'She never gets up before breakfast.' In one graceful movement he slid down beside her, lying full length on his stomach, his chin cupped in long brown fingers on raised elbows while he gazed at her. He was so near that she could see the length of his incredible black eyelashes and had to quell an almost irresistible desire to touch them.

'Let us introduce ourselves,' he said lazily. 'What's your name?'

'Audrey Winter,' she told him mechanically.

'A pretty name,' and she had had an odd impression that it wasn't unknown to him. 'Are you alone?'

'Oh no, but my friend isn't up yet.'

'The girl I saw you with? The hungry-eyed harpy?'

'That's unkind! Cheryl isn't a harpy.'

'Definitely one. I know that type ... young men, beware!' His eyes were on her hair with a sensuous gleam in their dark depths. Impatiently she swept it back.

'My hair's a nuisance,' she told him. 'I'm thinking of having it cut off.'

'Don't you dare, that would be sheer vandalism.' He reached out and touched a stray lock. 'Fine as silk.'

She whisked it away. 'You haven't told me your name,' she reminded him, 'Mr ... er ...?'

'Damon—there are no Misters on a cruise ship. Are you being deliberately provocative?'

'Certainly not.' Her wide grey eyes were ingenuous. 'I wouldn't know how.'

'It comes naturally to most women.'

'I've a feeling you despise women.'

'On the contrary, I admire them immensely, but I never cease to be amazed by feminine persistence in pursuit.'

Audrey drew away from him, finding his proximity disturbing and his words annoying. She had never met sex appeal in full blast before, and she had to admit that he would have an irresistible fascination, for women and modern girls were becoming too blatant where their desires were concerned. He had recognised poor Cheryl as a predator, but he was quite safe from herself. She would never allow herself to fall for Damon-Adonis, as no doubt he expected.

'I would never run after a man,' she announced confidently.

'Ah, but you're not fully fledged,' he told her, to her further annoyance. 'And by the time you are, some man may have caught you and saved you the necessity.'

'Pleasant prospect,' she jeered. 'So you allow that the chase isn't all one-sided?'

'Certainly not, but men should be permitted to do the hunting, which is their natural instinct.'

Other people were beginning to emerge on deck in various stages of nudity, prepared for sunbathing and swimming. Audrey stood up, feeling she needed her breakfast, and remarked that the deck was becoming

28

populated and he had better have his swim while there was still room.

He raised himself on his hands, looking up at her with eloquent dark eyes.

'But we'll meet again? I'll look out for you.'

'I'll be with my friend,' she said primly.

'Can't you dispose of her?'

'I don't want to, and what about Daphne?'

'I'm not wholly committed to her,' he told her.

Audrey remembered the other girl's possessive hand upon his arm.

'Perhaps you've led her to believe so, and I'm not a poacher.'

He grinned. 'I assure you I'm a free agent—at present.'

Which might mean that until Daphne's claim upon him became official he considered he was at liberty to follow his fancies.

'I'm afraid you're fickle,' she said with mock severity.

His eyes gleamed wickedly. 'Try me, you might be lucky.'

'No, thank you, I don't care for experiments,' she retorted.

'How unenterprising!' he scoffed, and springing to his feet, jumped into the pool.

Audrey picked up her towel and pattered away over the deck to the glass doors that gave admission to the other parts of the ship. She didn't believe in Damon's assumption of future contacts. Obviously he had had a tiff with his Daphne and was seeking other diversions, but he would go back to her in the end. Cheryl would be furious when she learned what she had missed by staying in bed; she regarded Damon as the most exciting man on the ship. Then, as she descended the stairs, Audrey decided to keep their encounter to herself. It was nothing to do with her friend, and since coming aboard she had been a little put off Cheryl. She hadn't realised she was

29

quite so man-mad. She had always been amused by her quick tongue and amusing comments but she did not want to have to listen to the ill-natured witticisms about herself and Damon with which she was sure Cheryl would seek to conceal her chagrin, especially as she was doubtful if he would bother to speak to her again when he had been reunited with his blonde.

As Mrs Archer had warned them, boat drill took place at ten o'clock. They were given their instructions over the tannoy and followed the directing arrows to their stations at the sound of the siren. Audrey fervently hoped that no emergency would arise, for she could not believe that the flood of passengers who trooped up laughing and joking, struggling with their cumbersome lifejackets to stand in rows on the deck for inspection, would do other than panic if confronted by the real thing. Possibly she misjudged them, but she had no desire to have her fears proved wrong.

The whole day was spent cruising down the Adriatic between the Italian and the Dalmatian coasts with never a sight of land. Nor did there seem to be much shipping about, and the *Andromeda* glided serenely along between an immensity of sky and a wide expanse of sea.

Most of the passengers spent the day stretched out in the sun, slowly broiling, white bodies turning red despite vigorous oiling. The ship's shop opened and so did the library. Some of the more energetic passengers played deck tennis or ping-pong. Cheryl still had her Beverley in tow, though she was seeking for younger game. Audrey changed a traveller's cheque for drachmae, which was the currency used on the ship, bought postcards and stamps at the Purser's office, took out a book, sunbathed a little and tried to persuade herself that she was not looking out for Damon, but every time she glimpsed a brown body and black head her heart gave a jump. But she did not see him again, though she did catch a glimpse of the lovely Daphne reclining on deck in the scantiest of bikinis, but he was not in attendance.

That evening the female portion of the passengers blossomed into their evening dresses. The Captain was holding his cocktail party in the largest of the lounges, or rather two parties, one for each sitting. Cheryl was provocative in a scarlet pyjama suit with wide flimsy trousers and a bodice composed of gold straps, and with her dark hair she looked oriental. Audrey wore a long green sheath that left her arms and shoulders bare, with an overdress of flimsy chiffon. Most of the women were draped in open-stitch shawls, for the air-conditioning was pleasantly cool. Audrey's, instead of the prevailing white, was of light green in heavy mesh silk. Both dress and shawl had been bought with Matthew's money, and so also had the amber necklace and bracelet that adorned neck and wrist.

They were lined up and processed solemnly into the lounge, where the Captain equally solemnly shook each by the hand. Then they passed down the line of ship's officers, resplendent in white mess jackets, who bowed and smiled. Finally they were presented with a glass of drink and allowed to disperse.

Audrey subsided on to a low seat in the middle of the room, having lost sight of Cheryl, who seemed mesmerised by the officers' mess kit. All around her was the buzz of talk, but though she had spoken to many people during the day she did not see anyone she knew in her immediate vicinity. She was making up her mind to address the man seated on her left, a somewhat dour-looking personage, when another man shouldered his way through the crowd and stood before her.

'May I?' he asked, indicating a vacant seat on her right, and without waiting for her permission dropped into it.

Damon had done honour to the Captain's reception by

31

dressing up. He was immaculately clad in white jacket and dark trousers, the curl in his black hair severely subdued, his cheeks shaved smooth. Involuntarily Audrey's heart began to beat faster. She looked around for Daphne, but he seemed to be alone. He held a wine-glass in his hand and over its brim he was regarding the proceedings with sardonic amusement.

'Poor Simonides must get a bit tired of going through this ceremony during the season,' he remarked. 'He was in command of the *Heracles* all last year, and a cruise vessel returns only to go out again with a fresh bunch week after week. But he's a patient soul and considers it part of the job. I should reach the pitch of wanting to throw cocktails into their gawping faces.'

'You aren't very polite to your fellow passengers.'

'Unfortunately they aren't all like you. You look charming tonight, Audrey, though I prefer you with less on.'

His audacious glance raked her slight figure, from the top of her ash-blonde head to her silver sandals. She wore her hair piled somewhat precariously on top of her head, and the style revealed the delicate contours of her head and throat. An expression of lazy appreciation came into his eyes as he raised the glass he held.

'To our closer acquaintanceship, and may it . . . ripen.'

Audrey leaned back in her seat, wishing he did not affect her so strongly with those black eyes of his, and they were so dark that the iris was indistinguishable from the pupil and played havoc with her senses when he looked at her in that sensuous manner.

'What are you aiming for, Damon,' she asked, 'a ship-board romance?' and hoped she sounded nonchalant.

'Isn't that what all you girls desire? Your primary object, in fact?'

'Not in my case. My chief interest is the ports of call, places I've read so much about and never expected to see.' Eagerness crept into her voice. 'Heraklion, Athens, Istanbul, the very names are magical.'

'Then let us hope they come up to your expectations.' He regarded her quizzically. 'Is this your first cruise?'

She had not meant to betray that fact, but apparently she had, and she said a little tartly:

'Of course you couldn't understand the thrill of it. You must be an experienced traveller.'

'It's my business, otherwise I wouldn't choose to be mixed up with this mob.'

Her eyes widened with interest. 'So you're something to do with the ship?'

He shrugged his shoulders. 'Unofficially, but don't spread that around. I don't want to be pestered with questions.' He put his glass on the tray of a passing waiter. 'It's getting hot in here. What about a stroll on deck?'

'But should we leave? The Captain ...'

'Won't notice your absence. Come and look at the moon on the Adriatic.' He sprang to his feet and held out his hand to her.

Audrey laid hers in it and a thrill shot up her arm at the touch of his long brown fingers. When she was on her feet he changed his hold to cup her elbow, guiding her expertly through the throng. She did not see Cheryl anywhere, nor the mysterious Daphne. Could the last be indisposed, and was that why Damon had appropriated her as a temporary stand-in? She could not suppose that he had abandoned such sophisticated loveliness in favour of her unremarkable self. They passed through the glass doors on to the after-deck where a noisy crowd was congregated round the bar. The pool was netted over for the night, and the stern of the ship was outlined in coloured lights. Damon guided her firmly up to the promenade deck, and she clutched her long skirts in her free hand to avoid stumbling on the steps. Here the noise below came to them muted and the lines of deck chairs were deserted ... almost ... a few couples intent upon closer union had sought seclusion among them. Damon led her up again to the boat deck which was dimly lit and quiet. On either side the sea reached to the horizon, above a silver moon shone placidly in a cloudless sky, and behind the ship a trail of phosphorescence marked her passage. The air was soft and balmy after the heat of the lounge.

'Tomorrow we make Corfu,' Damon observed as they leant over the rail. 'I suppose you've booked on the excursion to the Achilleion?'

'It seemed wiser, since we're novices, and what's wrong with the Achilleion?' She marked the contempt in his tone.

'Second-rate and boring,' he returned, 'it isn't the real Corfu. Couldn't you skip it and let me show you round?'

For a moment she was tempted, and then common-sense took command. She did not know anything about him and she distrusted him.

'I couldn't desert my friend,' she said demurely.

'Such estimable loyalty,' he gibed. 'In similar circumstances she wouldn't hesitate to desert you.'

Audrey winced, knowing that that was only too true, and he went on :

'You're neglecting your opportunities, my girl.'

'Meaning you consider yourself one?'

'Of course, but I don't neglect mine.'

She might have known it would happen, and she had half expected it would when she had agreed to come on deck, but she was not prepared for the ardour of his embrace nor the violence of her reaction to it. He held her close against the hard lean length of him, his knee thrust between her thighs, and the urgency of his mouth filled her veins with fire. No man had ever roused her to

34

such a pitch of melting surrender before, in fact she had never been roused at all. Far from being repelled she wanted him to go on and on, and he seemed in no hurry to let her go.

When at length he did release her he was breathing hard and she was trembling, then he took a handkerchief from his pocket and carefully wiped his face. The action disconcerted her—no novice he, he was anxious to remove any trace of lipstick she might have left upon him; actually she had used very little.

'You haven't been kissed before.' It was a statement, not a question.

Nettled by this suggestion of naïveté, she said sharply:
'Of course I have.'

'Kids' caresses,' he sneered, further incensing her.

'It's no business of yours,' she flashed.

'You think not?' he asked surprisingly, adding with seeming inconsequence, 'I like my roses with the bloom still on them.'

'Your tastes are a matter of indifference to me,' she returned, marvelling at her composed voice, for her pulses were still hammering. 'I believe you're a dangerous man, Damon, and I should keep clear of you.'

He laughed mockingly. 'Afraid?'

'Not so you'd notice.' But she was afraid of her physical response to him, and he was too practised, too assured; she was no match for him. 'But it must be getting very late,' she went on hurriedly, 'so I'll say goodnight, Damon.'

She moved towards the steps and he followed her.

'Why do you want to leave me just when we were getting to know each other?'

Poised above the stairs, she said disdainfully:

'There's some knowledge one is better without.'

He put a detaining hand on her arm. 'Oh, come now, what's in a kiss?'

35

'Oh, nothing, nothing at all,' she spoke a little wildly, 'but it's time I went.'

'Then say goodnight properly.'

He was drawing her into his arms again, but she resisted him, her body taut and rigid.

'No, Damon, please!'

His eyes showed a gleam of impatience in the moonlight.

'Don't be so damned prudish. You know you liked it.'

'Enough is enough. Please let me go.'

'Not until you pay ransom.'

Suddenly she was angry. He was making her feel cheap. She suspected he kissed every girl who took his fancy—his passing fancy—and expected his favours to be received with grateful rapture. Freeing one arm, she aimed a blow at his face. He caught her wrist before she could reach it, and his hand was like a steel manacle about it.

'A slapped face is a provocation no man who is a man can ignore,' he warned her. 'Had you carried out your intention I'd have made you pay for it, but as your effort failed . . .' He twisted her wrist, hurting her, then dropped it. 'Goodnight, Miss Prim.'

He walked away from her, and the dismissal was so curt that she stood staring blankly after his retreating figure. Then, recollecting herself, she gathered up her long skirt preparatory to descent.

'Goodnight, Damon,' she called over her shoulder. 'I'll forgive you.'

Her words surprised him and he turned back.

'Forgive . . . me!'

'For being fresh. Sweet dreams.'

She sped lightly back to the after-deck, resisting an impulse to look back to see if he were following. She did not pause until she reached the crowd and the bright lights. Then she did look up. He was standing at the rail above her, too far away for her to see his expression, but he appeared to be watching her. She waved her hand and passed from his sight.

In the lounge she subsided into one of the low comfortable chairs, more shaken by the experience than she wanted to admit. It was not the lounge where the Captain's party had taken place but a smaller one, reserved for those who wished to be quiet, and she needed its peace to restore her shattered nerves. She was used to casual kisses from boy-friends, they were common currency nowadays. Kids' caresses, Damon had called them, but there had been nothing casual about Damon's embrace, it had been full of intention. He was a man and an experienced one, and it was possible his purpose was seduction, a shipboard romance carried to its logical conclusion. To that she would never consent, but he would be hard to resist with her own body fighting on his side. Cheryl might not be so particular, but Audrey had too much self-respect to succumb to the first foreign wolf who made overtures to her, for whatever else he was Damon was not English.

Moreover, there was Daphne, whose rôle in his life she had not yet been able to determine. She knew nothing about him, not even his surname, except for his hint that he was there in some official capacity. But surely it was not good business to be so scornful of his clients, as he was towards the other passengers? He probably scorned her, too, for being so easily available. She knew that a lot of girls went on holiday with the intention of picking up a presentable male to share the fun, but she did not care for that sort of fun. Her face burned as she recalled her eager acceptance of Damon's kisses, and the fact that her blood raced at the memory did not lessen her sense of shame. She must avoid him in future, but that would not be difficult, he would keep out of her way after her snub.

37

'Can I get you a drink?'

She started out of her reverie to encounter a pair of blue eyes in a boyish, unmistakably English face looking down at her with concern.

'Aren't you feeling too good?' the youth went on. 'A sherry or some such might pull you together.'

'I'm quite all right.' She smiled brightly. 'It's just that the heat and the noise brought on a headache.' And Damon, she added silently. 'I'll go below now.'

'Oh, please don't go, or at least have a drink with me first,' the boy pleaded. 'They've a concoction here called a grasshopper, it's smooth and creamy, though I don't know what's in it. Shall we try one together?' He beckoned to a passing waiter.

Audrey acquiesced. She did feel she needed a drink and this ingenuous youth was harmless. He sat down opposite to her and paid for the drinks when they arrived with an air of importance that amused her. Buying a drink for a girl was obviously a novel experience for him. His name, he told her, was Jimmy Brett, and he was accompanying his mother and sister, both of whom had retired overcome by the Captain's cocktails. This was his first cruise and everything was super.

'Do you know,' he told her in an awestruck tone, 'there's one old couple here who've been on fourteen cruises, and they're quite ordinary people too.'

'I suppose it could become a habit,' she observed, smiling, 'if one could afford it.'

'I'm surprised they can, but they say they've few expenses and there's no point in saving money that depreciates every year.' Jimmy looked very solemn. 'But cruising gets more expensive every year, and there'll be no more cheap ones.'

'That'll be hard on your elderly couple.'

'Oh well, they'll have plenty to look back on, but let's talk about you. Are you alone?'

38

Audrey explained about Cheryl, guiltily aware that she hadn't seen her since dinner.

'I'm sorry about that,' Jimmy looked disappointed. 'I hoped we could be friends.'

Audrey suspected he was younger than she was and compared to Damon he appeared a mere infant, but he could be a bulwark against the elder man's advances; that was, if Damon made any more.

'We're not inseparable,' she explained, 'there's no reason why you and I shouldn't be friends. Do you swim?'

He complained about the pool being overcrowded. .

'It isn't first thing in the morning.'

The upshot was that they fixed a rendezvous at the pool next morning at seven-thirty. Fortified by the grasshopper, Audrey reflected triumphantly that if Damon did appear then he would find she had acquired a less demanding escort. She left Jimmy with a pleasant feeling of having somehow scored off that enigmatical personality.

Cheryl was absent when she reached their cabin, nor did she come down until long after Audrey was asleep.

Waking early, Audrey saw from the window a grey land mass and realised that Corfu must be in sight. She sprang out of bed excitedly and shook Cheryl's shoulder, but her friend merely gave a protesting grunt and turned over. Audrey paid no more attention to her, but hastily put on her swimsuit and towelling wrap, seized a towel and her bathing cap and ran up on deck.

The forward half of the after-deck was enclosed by awnings on either side to protect it from sun and wind, but beyond the pool it was open to the sky. Even so, a still better view could be obtained from the promenade deck, and Audrey ran up the steps to avail herself of it.

On one side she saw the misty heights of Albania, that mysterious country that had closed its frontiers when it adopted Communism. On the other was the mountainous northern end of Corfu. It was still too far away to distinguish much detail, and remembering Jimmy, she put on her cap and went back to the pool.

He was there waiting for her but not alone.

'My kid sister, Kathy,' he said disgustedly indicating a leggy fourteen-year-old. 'She insisted on coming.'

'The pool's free to all, isn't it?' Kathy gave Audrey an engaging grin. She was blue-eyed like her brother and both had snub noses and freckles. 'I didn't see why I shouldn't come along if you're going to swim, and it's too early in the day for necking.'

She glanced impishly at Jimmy.

'Don't be daft,' he said, flushing, and pushed her into the pool. She went in with a splash and he turned to Audrey, 'After you, madam,' and Audrey descended into the water more sedately.

The two youngsters gambolled like puppies, splashing and ducking each other. Audrey forgot her adult dignity and joined in the romp. She lost her cap and her wet hair got into her eyes, and other people besides the Bretts entered the pool. Somebody grabbed her legs and pulled her under the water, heedless of her spluttering protests; then she felt herself being lifted on to the rim of the pool. Springing to her feet and pushing her hair off her face, she beheld Damon standing in front of her and laughing.

'How dare you interfere!' she cried furiously, overwhelmed by the realisation that it was he who had ducked her and his arms had raised her. 'I was having fun.'

He sobered. 'Do you really enjoy such juvenile antics?' he asked contemptuously. 'Come and see what you're missing.'

He took hold of her arm and pulled her off the edge of the pool and marched her towards the stern. The island was much clearer now, and she could distinguish the rocky headlands and wooded hills below an impressive height.

'Mount Pantokrator,' Damon told her, 'and this is about the best view you'll get of it. Your trip will take you south.'

'I did have a look earlier on, but everything was misty,' she said defensively.

'And then you became distracted by your infant cavalier?'

'You shan't jeer at Jimmy, he's nice.'

She was painfully conscious that he had put his arm about her waist to clamp her to his side. The contact of their bare skins were causing tremors to run up her spine and she hardly knew what she was saying. Since he made no comment upon her defence of Jimmy, she went on desperately:

'Thank you for showing me the mountain, but now I must go and dress, we'll be coming into port.' She tried ineffectively to disengage herself, and his arm tightened.

'No hurry, we shan't dock for an hour or more.'

Houses were visible along the shore line and sailing boats on the blue water. The remote mountains of Albania were retreating. Audrey tried to concentrate on the scenery, but she was distracted by the sensations Damon was arousing in her.

The Bretts came running up beside them.

'Oo-er!' Kathy cried, 'What a lovely place!' She hung over the rail. Jimmy was looking at Audrey reproachfully.

'I thought you were going to be my girl,' he blurted out, and then to Audrey's relief, Damon removed his arm as he turned to face the boy. She expected that he would make some cutting remark, but he smiled brilliantly and said mildly:

'She's a little old for you.'

Jimmy drew himself up proudly. 'I'm eighteen, sir.'

Involuntarily he gave Damon this title of respect. 'And I'm sure she isn't much older. You're ... er ... a bit mature, aren't you? I mean, you're not in the same age bracket.'

'Perhaps not,' Damon did not seem at all offended. 'But a woman's husband should be older than herself.'

'Good gracious,' Audrey exclaimed, 'whoever's thinking of husbands?'

Damon's smile became sardonic. 'Doesn't every woman view each man she meets through the circle of a wedding ring?' he inquired suavely.

'What a horrid thing to say! I assure you this one doesn't.'

Kathy, who had detached herself from the landscape to stare at Damon, now intervened.

'I think you're absolutely smashing, and of course Audrey's gone on you. I shall be myself.'

'Thank you,' Damon said gently, looking down into her candid eyes. 'I'm not worthy of your innocent admiration.'

Hypocrite, Audrey thought, I bet he thrives on female adulation. Aloud she said: 'You're all being quite absurd, and it's time we made a move if we want to be ready to go ashore.'

Someone had retrieved her cap and thrown it on to the broad rim of the pool. She went to collect it and her towel and wrap, slipping her arms into the last. Looking back, she saw the three by the rail were standing in a row watching her. Jimmy's eyes were admiring and Kathy's curious, but Damon's gaze was a hard penetrating stare that struck a chord of memory. With just such an expression of cool appraisal Matthew Gregory had regarded her when he had made known to her his plan for her holiday. It was of him Damon reminded her, their eyes were alike and so was their way of standing.

Now as then she felt chilled. Could there possibly be a connection between them?

Then she recalled that Matthew was half Greek. The resemblance, if there was one and it was not her fancy evoked by similar dark eyes, was one of nationality, nothing more. Reassured, she waved her hand to the trio and ran towards the exit.

Kathy caught her as she opened the door.

'You're going on the excursion, aren't you? May I sit next to you in the coach?'

'I don't know, you see I've a friend with me.'

Kathy's face fell. 'Him?' She jerked her head in Damon's direction.

'Certainly not. Cheryl is a girl.'

Kathy brightened. 'Then she can sit with Jimmy. You don't mind?'

'No, but Jimmy might,' Audrey said drily, knowing that Cheryl would regard her youthful admirer as a schoolboy and beneath her notice.

'You mustn't let him monopolise you,' said Miss Fourteen sagely. 'I can see he's not your type, and you'll find him a nuisance if you encourage him.'

'I don't think I'll do that,' Audrey said, laughing, 'we'll just have to see, won't we?'

She would be glad to have Kathy's company and she certainly didn't want to give Jimmy too much encouragement. It would not be fair when she ... even to herself she would not acknowledge that there was somebody else whose society would have been more attractive. After his scornful remarks Damon would not be going near the Achilleion, and she had refused his offer to show her the real Corfu, which she doubted had been serious. Though she had eagerly anticipated the excursion it no longer seemed so enjoyable.

As she went along the corridor to her cabin a familiar figure came towards her. Daphne was dressed for going

ashore in a white embroidered dress with a blue crino-
line hat. She looked beautiful and aloof and went past
Audrey with a disparaging glance at her tangled hair.

Audrey felt sure, with a sickening certainty, that she
was going with Damon. She wondered why the knowledge made her feel so depressed.

CHAPTER THREE

By the time she was ready to disembark, Audrey's spirits had risen; she was eager to leave the ship and see what was to be seen. The waterfront with its background of gardens looked enticing. Corfu town—or Kerkyra—was at the southern end of the sickle-shaped bay that curved into the north-east section of the island, and part of it was built on a rocky promontory. The *Andromeda* had berthed at the quayside and lowered her gangway, and her passengers streamed down it to be ushered into the fleet of coaches drawn up waiting for them. The two Bretts had found Audrey and attached themselves to her, and Cheryl accepted their presence with bored indifference. In the coach she sat beside Audrey, and they installed themselves in the seats across the gangway. Mrs Archer and Miss Green were behind them.

'Lord, what a set-up,' Cheryl whispered. 'Might as well be on a Sunday School outing!'

Audrey hoped her remark had not been overheard; she was quite content with her company—well, almost. She resolutely pushed all thought of Damon out of her mind.

It was a hot and sunny day, sky and sea a deep blue, the buildings mostly white and red-roofed and delightfully foreign-looking, but in retrospect Audrey could only recall a few outstanding features of her morning in Corfu. There was too much to assimilate on one brief visit. The horse-drawn carriages with their canopies, the animals wearing straw hats, stuck in her memory. There was a row of them waiting for hire beyond the landing stage, but their courier warned them that their cost was prohibitive. She received a vague impression of the two Venetian forts each on a rocky rise, former guardians of the town's security. They were driven past a low-lying lagoon and the distant airfield, and she could see that the island was densely wooded, olive trees predominating with among them the dark spires of cypresses.

The Achilleion made a deeper impression. It was reached up a steep twisting road. A white Italianate palace, it had been rescued from decay by the government to be hired out as a casino, but the lower rooms were accessible to the public and had been turned into a museum. There were relics of the ill-fated Empress Elizabeth for whom it had been built, and a portrait of her by Winterhalter. Not that she had ever stayed there long, she never remained anywhere for long until an assassin stayed her wandering feet for ever.

The palace stood on a hill amid beautiful grounds at different levels, with a spectacular view over the sea. There were two statues of Achilles in the garden and a large picture of his victory over Hector in one of the rooms. Why the place had been dedicated to the Homeric hero nobody seemed to know. Museums, Audrey decided, were all right on wet days, but a waste of time when the sun was shining. She and the Bretts escaped into the rear courtyard with its pillared colonnade adorned with second-rate statues of the nine Muses, its tall palm trees and masses of bougainvillea. They sat down on the marble steps and waited for the rest of the party to join them.

'The Greek tyrant doesn't seem to be with us,' Jimmy remarked, watching the flight of a swallow-tailed butterfly, a rarity in England. He had been checking up on the bus loads.

'Why do you call him that?' Audrey asked, knowing very well whom he meant.

'They called V.I.P.s tyrants in ancient Greece, and I've

46

a hunch he's one. He's always chatting up the Captain or being matey with the cruise manager. His full name's Damon Grivas.'

'You seem very well informed.' Audrey strove to speak casually, and not betray undue interest.

'Oh, Jimmy's a regular sleuth, and Damon does rather stick out,' Kathy chipped in. 'We'd noticed him before he joined us this morning, and we like to know who's who.' She sighed. 'I'm afraid I made no impression.'

'What, a kid like you?' her brother jeered. 'But watch your step, Audrey, he's a prowling pussy, that one, for all he's deeply involved with that snotty blonde. She's a Mrs Remington-Smythe, by the way. Double-barrelled names stink of snobbishness.'

'They do rather,' Audrey agreed, 'but is she a widow?'

Kathy shrugged her thin shoulders. 'That's anybody's guess, but there isn't a Mr Remington-Smythe on the passenger list.'

That document was posted in reception, and evidently the Bretts had been studying it, but it hadn't occurred to Audrey to do so.

'I've taken Mr Grivas' measure,' she said loftily, glad that Jimmy did not know about the episode on the boat deck. 'I won't let him put anything over me. He's not with us today because he scorns organised excursions.'

'He would,' Jimmy declared. 'Bet you he's gone off to some expensive hotel with his blonde in tow.'

'We shan't miss him, shall we?' Audrey inquired with false brightness, wondering where Damon would have taken her if she had accepted his invitation, but of course he could not have really meant it.

'Not bloody likely,' Jimmy said, quoting Eliza Dolittle.

The rest of the party came straggling towards them, the guide giving the three truants disapproving looks, and they moved on.

47

Loaded into the coaches again, they were driven to the wooded village of Kanoni, the rural atmosphere of which place was being rapidly destroyed by the erection of new hotels. Here on the cliff above the sea was a souvenir shop and a café, to the delight of Mrs Archer and her sister, who had an insatiable appetite for postcards.

'And we'll have a lemonade at the café while we write them,' Miss Green said happily. But Audrey and her friends preferred more active pursuits. They had been told they could visit the little monastery of Vlacherna, which they could see below them in the sea, connected to the mainland by a narrow paved causeway. They went racing down the steep wooded path that led to it, Cheryl accompanying them. Arrived there, they congratulated themselves upon wearing summer dresses, for two girls in bikinis were sternly refused admittance by the guardian nun. The little red-roofed building with its belfry and one tall cypress tree must have been an ideal place for contemplation, surrounded as it was by water before it became commercialised, even now its bare walls retained something of its old-time serenity. Jimmy, glancing at his watch, announced that they'd have to scram to get the coach, and as they hurried back up the partly stepped ascent, Audrey wished they were allowed longer to explore. She thought a little wistfully of Damon's offer.

On the way back her attention was caught by a gorgeous tree of blue and mauve blossom while the coach was halted by a traffic sign. 'Oh, what is it?' she gasped.

'Jacaranda,' said Miss Green from behind her.

'Jacaranda—lovely name. I've often read about them, and now I've actually seen one.'

'It's only an old tree,' Jimmy observed contemptuously. 'You'll see much more interesting things than that.'

But Audrey loved all trees and plants, and she continued to gaze rapturously at the blue blossom until the coach moved on again.

They were finally dumped beside the cricket ground and told they had half an hour to shop. Corfu is the only place in Greece where cricket is played, being a legacy from the brief British occupation of the island. The British, too, were responsible for the Royal Palace, to-day another museum, which flanked the pitch. Along one side was the Liston Arcade with its rows of arches sheltering shops and cafés, and behind it the network of narrow streets that comprised the old town. Audrey and Cheryl wandered through them, but the Bretts had stopped for ice cream and were left behind. They gazed at displays of basketware, Grecian pottery, jewellery, lace and other craft work. In a slightly wider street, cars nosed their way through, and several barrows offered a tempting display of fruit. Audrey heard the clip-clop of hooves, and looking up saw Daphne and Damon seated side by side in one of the Victorias she had seen near the quay, drawn by its bonneted horse. Damon as well as his inamorata was wearing white, a silk shirt and trousers. The canopy shaded their faces, but Audrey could see that his dark head was inclined towards her fair one as if he were absorbed in what she was saying.

Her attention thus diverted, Audrey was not looking where she was going and she collided with one of the fruit barrows drawn up by the kerb. Peaches, cherries and strawberries went cascading into the gutter, and while she stared in horror at what she had done, its owner scolded her in an unknown tongue. Several other people collected, arguing and gesticulating, some in her defence, others supporting the owner. Scarlet with embarrass-ment, Audrey stammered an apology and made an in-effectual attempt to pick up some of the scattered fruit. Cheryl had walked on, pretending she did not know her, and the Bretts were still imbibing ice cream.

A sudden silence fell on the noisy group, and she looked round nervously, expecting to see a policeman, and beheld to her astonishment Damon standing beside her, lithe and debonair, a little ironic smile on his lips. She could not have been more surprised or relieved if the Angel Gabriel had appeared to deliver her.

He dismissed the barrow man with a few words in Greek and a handful of drachmae. Then, cupping her elbow with his hand, he led her away from the scene of her crime.

'Corfiotes are not often so discourteous to strangers,' he observed. 'It was obviously an accident, but fruit can be ruined by being bruised and the stuff is the fellow's living.'

'Thank you for rescuing me,' Audrey murmured. 'I'm not usually so clumsy. I can't think what distracted me.'

But she did know very well and she looked round for the carriage, but it had disappeared. Cheryl, seeing what had happened, came running after them. Audrey stopped as she came up to them and withdrew her arm from Damon's light clasp. Her friend was eyeing him avidly.

'Thank you, thank you so much,' Cheryl gasped; she was a little out of breath, and Damon raised his brows, glancing questioningly at Audrey. 'Audrey was daydreaming,' Cheryl went on, 'and not looking where she was going. It's a bad habit of hers. We're very grateful to you. That fellow looked as if he might become nasty.'

'And that was why you walked on?' Damon inquired suavely.

Cheryl was quite unabashed. 'I was going to find our courier,' she explained, 'to sort things out.'

Damon looked unimpressed and Audrey intervened hastily.

'This is my friend Cheryl, we're travelling together. Cheryl, this is Mr Grivas.' Damon again raised his brows at the surname which he himself had not disclosed.

50

'You've seen him on the *Andromeda*,' Audrey continued.

'Yes, of course, and being on the same cruise constitutes an introduction, doesn't it?' Cheryl batted her eyelids and smiled coyly. 'I couldn't overlook you, you're so distinguished and most of the passengers are so ordinary.'

Damon smiled wryly. 'That's their misfortune, not their fault, and with such a crowd one can't possibly get to know everybody. By great good fortune I met your friend by the swimming pool.'

'So that's why you've been getting up so early!' Cheryl cried. She looked accusingly at Audrey. 'It wasn't to meet those kids, you sly creature! I'd get up early too with such an inducement.'

Aware of Damon's mocking glance, Audrey could have hit her, but he said kindly:

'Audrey doesn't get up early on my account, she hopes to find the pool empty so she can frolic with her young companions.'

He made them sound like teenagers, which of course the Bretts were. She said coldly, 'Mr Grivas has his own friends.' Turning to Damon, she asked: 'By the way what's happened to Mrs Remington-Smythe?'

'You have been doing your homework,' he exclaimed. 'Daphne has evidently become tired of waiting.'

'Oh dear, and it's all my fault.' Audrey was genuinely contrite. 'Will she be all right?'

He shrugged his shoulders. 'She can look after herself. She's done her shopping and she will have gone back to the ship.'

Daphne the cool and confident would never blunder into fruit barrows, and would always be able to extricate herself gracefully from awkward situations, Audrey thought sadly.

'I remember now,' Cheryl cried, 'when we saw you on

51

deck on the first day; Daphne was that glamorous girl who was with you.' She did not hesitate to use Mrs Remington-Smythe's first name. She shot a barbed glance at Audrey, annoyed because she hadn't disclosed that she had become acquainted with such attractive people, but Audrey was not attending. She was looking round, hoping to see someone she knew from the ship who would break up this three-cornered conversation which was making her feel uncomfortable. That she would have to face Cheryl's cross-examination when they were alone—and she did not want to discuss Damon with her—was bad enough, and she feared what other revelations he might make. There was a malicious gleam in his eyes which boded her no good. She did not think he liked Cheryl's reference to Daphne, and he might retaliate by making some embarrassing remark. Jimmy and his sister, whose intervention she would have welcomed, seemed to have disappeared.

'Possibly you did,' Damon answered Cheryl vaguely, not prepared to commit himself. He turned markedly to Audrey to the exclusion of her friend. 'Have you seen Saint Spiridon's shrine? It's the most characteristic thing in Corfu.'

'No, it wasn't included in our itinerary,' she told him. 'He's their patron saint or some such, isn't he?'

'Much more than that. He holds in his withered hands the destinies of all good Corfiotes. He keeps an eye on the shipping, the crops and I daresay the tourist trade.'

Audrey looked at him doubtfully, but he seemed to be perfectly serious except for a glimmer of mischief beneath his lowered lids.

'Silly nonsense,' Cheryl ejaculated.

'Be careful, it's not wise to offend the saint in his own habitat,' Damon warned her. To Audrey, he went on; 'Since he has so opportunely sent me to your rescue you must pay him a visit, it's only courteous. Come, I'll show you the way.' He laid his hand upon her arm.

'There isn't time,' Cheryl objected. 'The courier said we must be sure not to keep the coach waiting.'

'I won't let your friend miss the boat,' Damon assured her, thereby indicating that he hadn't included Cheryl in his invitation.

'But . . .' Audrey began, and he frowned.

'That's a word I dislike.'

She remembered Matthew Gregory had made a similar complaint. Both men had the same arrogant way of sweeping aside opposition.

'I'd love to see him,' she said eagerly, as much to keep Damon beside her as from any desire to see the shrine. 'May Cheryl come too?'

'No, thank you,' her friend declined huffily, peeved that Damon had not included her. 'I'm not interested in any old saint, and I'm not going to hold the coach for you if you're late either. You can find your own way back.' She stalked off with her head in the air.

'Aghios Spiridon doesn't welcome scoffers,' Damon observed as he conducted Audrey along a narrow street.

She said nothing. She could not credit that he really believed in any miraculous powers accruing to the fifteenth-century bishop's remains, nor could she understand why he was insisting upon taking her on this pilgrimage. It was enough for her that he had deserted Daphne and was prepared to act as her guide. Was she falling in love with this enigmatic Greek? she wondered. It was time that she did fall in love, real love as distinct from teenage crushes, she decided, and the contact of his hand upon her arm was both pleasant and exciting. Love was something she had not yet fully experienced, and she wanted to try everything at least once. That she had selected a somewhat dangerous object with which to experiment did flash through her mind, but did one have a choice? She was being directed by fate—or perhaps Saint Spiridon.

She was confused when they once more gained the bright street after those few moments beside the glass case surrounded by tapers—offerings of the devout—which contained the blackened, shrivelled mummy of the one-time bishop. She hadn't realised that she would be confronted by the actual body—not that there was anything macabre about it, it was oddly pathetic. Four times a year in his golden palanquin, Damon told her, he was carried round the town in solemn procession, and every second boy in Corfu was named after him.

'But surely modern people can't be so superstitious?' she asked.

'It isn't superstition, but simple faith,' Damon told her, 'something modern people are losing fast without anything to put in its place except the worship of Mammon. The humbler Corfiotes get a great deal of comfort from their belief in their saint. I envy them.'

She stared at him a little blankly, astonished by such observations coming from one who seemed to be so cynically sophisticated. Then automatically she glanced at her watch and gave an exclamation of dismay.

'I'll have to run to catch that coach!'

'You mustn't run in this heat. You'd melt, and there's not a lot of you to start with. Don't fret, we'll take a taxi and probably arrive before the coach.'

She hoped Cheryl would not be worried by her non-appearance, but after her threat this seemed unlikely, and she knew Audrey was with Damon.

In the taxi she thanked him for taking her to Aghios Spiridon. 'I find that sort of thing much more interesting than shopping,' she told him.

'I thought you might do, but you're in a minority.'

'I suppose so. I hope Mrs Remington-Smythe won't mind?'

The question was an artful one, but he did not rise.

'Why should she?' he queried. 'She doesn't appreciate Saint Spiro, and I always like to call upon him when I come to Corfu.'

'Of course, you're Greek, Mr Grivas,' she observed as if that explained him.

'But not a Corfiote.' He glanced at her quizzically. 'You've been checking up on me, haven't you?'

She coloured faintly. 'It was Jimmy, he's been consulting the passenger list.'

'He's the youth you were bathing with?'

'He's nice,' she said defensively.

'And I'm ... not?'

'You've been very nice ... today.' She emphasised the last word, and he laughed.

'Nice is an insipid adjective, and singularly inappropriate to describe myself.'

'I could use others,' she returned archly, 'but I do appreciate your kindness.'

He gave her a long enigmatic look. 'And you're a nice child,' he summed her up.

Audrey was nettled. She didn't want to appear as a child to him; he had been showing her round as he would a daughter or a niece, as Uncle Matt would have done.

'I'm nearly twenty-one,' she told him loftily.

'A vast age,' he mocked. 'I'm thirty, and I've had nine more years of life than you, *agape mou*, and I've lived them.'

'I can believe that,' she retorted drily wondering what *agape mou* meant. It was the first time she had heard him use a Greek word. He seemed determined to emphasise her naïveté, and compared with himself and Daphne she supposed she must appear very juvenile.

The taxi reached the quayside and she saw the white shape of the *Andromeda*, which already seemed like home. They had arrived ahead of the coaches and the open space was almost deserted as they walked towards the ship.

'One objection to a cruise is that you're always in a crowd,' she complained.

'You're not in a crowd now.'

'Yes, it's nice.'

'Nice again? Your vocabulary seems limited to *nice* and *but*.'

She glanced at him coquettishly. 'It also includes *no*.'

'Your English negative is the Greek affirmative; *né*,' he pronounced it *nay*, 'means yes, but if you mean what I think you mean, that's a pity. There'll be other ports and we could avoid the crowd.'

This sounded promising, but where did his blonde fit into the picture? She paused at the foot of the gangway and said deliberately:

'Would Mrs Remington-Smythe approve of that?'

'For God's sake call her Daphne,' he exclaimed irritably.

'I don't consider I'm on sufficiently intimate terms to do that,' she retorted. 'We haven't been introduced.'

'Introductions aren't necessary on a cruise ship,' he countered. '*We* weren't introduced.'

'If we had been your sponsor might have offered a word of explanation,' she suggested flippantly. 'I find you are full of contradictions, Mr Grivas, and something of an enigma.'

'A reversal of roles. Women are supposed to be the mysterious sex, though,' an edge crept into his voice, 'they're no mystery to me.'

The coaches were arriving and a wave of decanted passengers swept towards them.

'I suppose you consider you can read me like a book,' Audrey inquired, hoping he could not, 'but doesn't every human being have some uncut pages?'

'But yours, my darling, are still mostly blank,' he said softly.

My darling! But the endearment was used as if she were a child or a puppy. Audrey gave a little scornful shrug as the first passengers reached them, and ran lightly up the gangway. As she went she heard Cheryl's shrill voice as she caught up with Damon.

'So you've got here first after all. We thought you'd abducted Audrey.'

Well, Cheryl wouldn't get much change out of him.

The *Andromeda* sailed in the afternoon and Audrey stood at the rail on the after-deck watching the island recede. She had enjoyed her visit and it had been greatly enhanced by Damon's presence, but if she hadn't barged into the fruit barrow he would have driven past with Daphne without observing her. Cheryl believed that she had done it on purpose to attract his attention. She had been a little catty about the episode, but admitted that she admired what she termed Audrey's strategy that had paid off so handsomely.

'You're not as dumb as you look,' she had conceded.

Audrey forbore to protest that the mishap had been wholly genuine, since it had raised her in her friend's estimation, and wondered if Damon too doubted its genuineness. She did not think he would have come to her assistance if he had. But why *had* he been so keen to show her the island's saint? Did he want to test her reaction to the quaint superstition, but if so, again why? She was not vain enough to believe that he could be really attracted to her, not with the glamorous Daphne in the offing. Perhaps he had simply taken her on impulse, as he was going himself while Daphne preferred to return to the ship, and she would be foolish to attach any importance to his action. Corfu faded into a grey smudge on the horizon and she went below to change for dinner.

After the meal, feeling a little tired, she resisted the Bretts' attempts to persuade her to accompany them to the discothèque in the bowels of the ship, shrinking from the heat and the noise. Cheryl went with them, having heard that the off-duty ships' officers were sometimes to be found there, while Audrey betook herself to the Perseus Lounge, so-called because the murals on its walls depicted the story of Andromeda being rescued by him from the sea monster which was considered appropriate to the ship. It was reserved for those who wanted peace and quiet. A noisy crowd were gathered in the bigger lounge forward, where there was dancing and a cabaret, but the sound came muted through the closed glass doors. She sat by the window in one of the superbly comfortable chairs with which the lounge was furnished, gazing out at the sea illuminated by the waning moon. The few other occupants of the lounge seemed to have gone to sleep.

'So there you are, in maiden meditation, fancy-free!'

It was Damon, and her pulses leaped at the sound of his voice. She could never encounter him suddenly without an involuntary physical response.

'It's so nice here,' she explained, and recalled that he had objected to the repeated use of that adjective. 'Restful,' she amended hastily.

'So you're tired of the continual racket, and I sympathise. Let me get you a drink.'

That was the accepted formula when boy met girl on the *Andromeda*. As she was about to refuse, it occurred to Audrey that he would bring one for himself also and stay with her while he drank it. She could not miss such an opportunity.

'Thank you, I'd like a fruit cup with lots of ice,' she told him.

'Nothing stronger?'

'I ... I'm not all that keen on alcohol,' she admitted,

and wondered if she sounded very unsophisticated.

But he smiled approval, saying, 'Wise girl.'

He moved away from her to seek the bar and she watched his lithe supple figure cross the lounge with appreciative eyes. His cream jacket and trousers bore the stamp of an expensive tailor. Damon Grivas showed signs of affluence. It was remarkable that Daphne Remington-Smythe seemed so indifferent to him that she so frequently let him out of her sight, but perhaps they weren't lovers as she had assumed, but relations of some sort. She found the supposition cheering.

Damon returned with her fruit juice, and as she had expected a whisky for himself. He sat down in the chair opposite to her, grimacing as he did so.

'It's a long way down into these seats.'

'And quite an effort to get out of them. I don't want to move.'

'You needn't, need you?' There was a little table between them on which he had placed their glasses, and leaning back he lit a cigar.

'Now tell me all about yourself.'

Audrey had already received several life stories. People were curiously lacking in reticence, possibly because they knew they were unlikely to meet their listeners again, and to relate an autobiography was a pleasant way to while away relaxed hours in deck chairs, but she was not one of them. Her history up to now had been so uneventful.

'There's very little to tell,' she confessed. 'I'd much rather hear about you.'

'Ladies first,' he prevaricated. 'You live with your parents?'

'How did you guess?'

'You haven't got the hard gloss of the bachelor girl. I suspect you've always been sheltered and are not very enterprising.'

'In other words, dull?'

'I didn't say that. It's interesting to speculate how you're going to develop when you do strike out on your own.' He looked at her critically. 'You could be beautiful if you were groomed by experts.'

'Am I so plain now?' she asked, not liking the implication that she was dowdy.

'Don't put words into my mouth. That green thing you're wearing is becoming, but it's nothing to what haute couture could do for you.' He spoke with a proprietorial air, as if her embellishment were a matter of personal interest to him. 'Your eyes are wonderful, but your hair ...'

'I told you before it's a nuisance,' she interrupted him. 'The only way to deal with it is to cut it off, but you objected to that idea and so do my parents.'

'It only needs expert treatment.'

'Which would be expensive. Daphne has short hair.'

'I wouldn't want you to look like Daphne.'

'I couldn't, could I?' His observations were becoming too intimate, and his close scrutiny was also a little embarrassing, almost as if he had a personal stake in how she looked. She said reprovingly:

'It's very kind of you to be so interested in my appearance, Damon, but it isn't really anything to do with you. When this cruise is over I'll go back to my typewriter—I'm a stenographer—where haute couture would be most unsuitable. What will you be doing?'

She looked at him interrogatively.

He carefully removed the ash from the butt of his cigar, his eyes downcast so that his long eyelashes threw shadows on his cheeks. Again she wanted to touch them. Ignoring her query, he said:

'Unexpected things happen. It may be that your future is more involved with mine than you suspect.'

She did not know what to make of that remark—his

face was quiet and quite inscrutable. What was he suggesting?

'That isn't possible,' she declared.

'All things are possible.' He raised his eyes and met her candid gaze with a wry little smile. 'Have you any plans for your future when you've cut the parental apron strings?'

'I'm not tied to Mummy and Daddy, but I'm happy with them, so why should I want to live on my own? No, I've no plans, I'm not ambitious and I'm quite content with my daily round.'

'How pleasant to hear you say that! You've none of the restlessness and dissatisfaction that besets so many modern women, the insatiable greed for masculine admiration. You're so serene, Audrey.'

Intuitively she felt that he was deliberately probing her, but could not imagine what his motive could be.

'You'll make some man a good wife,' he concluded.

'I'm not thinking of getting married,' she informed him, 'in fact I don't mind being single at all. Marriage as far as I'm concerned is a very remote possibility.' She spoke all the more emphatically in case he imagined she had designs upon himself.

He met her eyes with a glint of amusement in the dark depths of his.

'But you're not frigid,' he told her, 'I ascertained that.' She blushed furiously, knowing to what he referred. 'If you don't marry, you'll have to have ... affairs.'

Was that what he was leading up to? But she would hesitate to have one with him, much as he attracted her. She sensed it would become too serious on her part, and though she was eager for experience, she didn't want to be hurt. Besides, there was Daphne.

'Not necessarily,' she said coldly. 'I've plenty of self-control.'

'Really?' Again she blushed, recalling how she had melted in his arms. 'Repression is bad for you,' he added.

'Not half as bad as over-indulgence,' she retorted. She looked at him warily. 'Are you trying to lead me astray, Damon?'

'God forbid!' he exclaimed so fervently that she was startled. 'I'm not a saint, Audrey, but I respect innocence. Keep yours as long as you can. That virginal air of yours becomes you, but it could be something of a challenge— to the wrong sort of man.'

'Thank you for the sermon,' she said tartly, not appreciating this description of herself at all. Innocence and virginal were insipid words to one who aspired to become a woman of the world. She had declared that she was in no haste to marry because she didn't want to become a housewife before she had had her fling, but she seemed to have misled him somehow. Probably because she had said she liked living at home, he thought she was a domesticated nitwit.

'What do you think I am?' she demanded. 'A child still?'

'In some ways, yes.'

'Compared with Mrs Remington-Smythe I suppose I must seem so, but she's got a long start of me, but when I'm her age ...'

He interrupted her, giving her a black look.

'We weren't discussing Daphne.'

'And I'd prefer that we cease to discuss me.' She half rose, but the chair defeated her and she sank back again. 'Are you going to Knossos?' she asked, striving to sound impersonal. 'It's a place I'm keen to see.'

He said he was. 'I'll take you,' he offered. 'I'll hire a car, it'll be pleasanter than travelling by coach. No ...' anticipating her question, 'Daphne doesn't care for ruins. She'll stay in Heraklion where we shall berth.'

'But haven't you seen it before?' she enquired.

'Yes, so I'll be an efficient guide.'

Audrey hesitated. She knew she would be wiser to refuse his invitation if she did not wish to become further involved with him, but he had all the fascination of playing with fire. The prospect of a car instead of the crowded coach and the pleasure—not to say excitement—of his company was very tempting.

He smiled wryly. 'I promise I won't do any more ... er ... experimenting with you, if that's what's worrying you.'

'Respecting my innocence?' she said scornfully.

'Isn't that what you wish?'

'Of course.' Which was not true. Now she had assurance that he would not attempt to kiss her again, for so she interpreted his words, something of the spice had gone out of their association. Regret must have shown in her face, for he laughed derisively.

'You're quite safe so long as you play fair. No sly incitement. I'm only human.'

A delicate colour suffused her face. He was altogether too astute, and it did not seem that his interest was avuncular.

Looking at him provocatively from under her eyelashes, she told him, 'You're a wily brute, Damon. What you're saying is that if ... er ... anything untoward occurs it'll be all my fault.'

'Naturally, it always is since Eve offered the first temptation. But of course you'll be entirely circumspect.' His black eyes were dancing with mischief; he was laughing at her.

Audrey drained the last of her fruit drink and said primly:

'I think I must refuse your escort.'

'Oh, don't do that!' His eyes challenged her. 'That would be a confession of weakness. Are you afraid your vaunted self-control might slip?'

'Oh, really,' Audrey laughed gaily. 'What rubbish we're talking!' Then naturally and frankly she accepted. 'Of course I'd love to come with you, Damon, and it's most kind of you to be prepared to show me round. I don't like official guides very much and I do dislike crowds.'

'Complete capitulation,' he declared with satisfaction. 'But don't go running away with the idea that I'm kind. That's another of your insipid words. I rarely do anything without good reason, and it's usually a selfish one.'

'Then may I ask what is your reason on this occasion?'

'Too complicated to explain,' he parried. 'Enough to say that I'll enjoy watching your reactions to the place and I find your company restful, especially as you don't expect me to make love to you.'

She nearly said 'and Daphne does', but bit back the words. She was not pleased by his last assertion. Was that why he had kissed her on the boat deck? He thought she'd expected it. Did he find his Daphne too demanding, and that was why he sought her out as an antidote?

These possibilities were not very flattering to her ego, but at least he had defined the situation between them. Neither wanted anything from the other except companionship. So she insisted to herself, restraining an insidious inner prompting that in reality she wanted a lot more. But not at the expense of her pride. A way to bolster it occurred to her.

'I suppose we couldn't take Jimmy and Kathy with us?' she suggested. 'Cheryl doesn't want to go on this excursion.'

That her friend had made plain at dinner when Mrs Archer and Miss Green had dilated upon what they hoped to see at Knossos.

'Certainly not,' Damon declared emphatically. 'I'd feel I was leading a Sunday School outing. You won't need a chaperone, haven't I made that clear?'

She smiled at the old-fashioned word. 'Chaperone my foot! We're in the nineteen-seventies. I only thought that if there were room in the car it was a pity to waste the space.'

'There will be only room for you and me,' he said firmly, and Audrey let the subject drop. Some instinct of self-preservation had prompted the suggestion, and Jimmy would be a useful foil to use if Damon became difficult. But she had much rather be alone with him, although she didn't altogether trust his promises, but danger would only make her outing more amusing. Recklessly she decided to follow her inclinations come what may. She was very thankful that Daphne Remington-Smythe did not like ruins.

CHAPTER FOUR

AUDREY sat on a block of stone at the side of the central court of King Minos' palace at Knossos. On the southern edge of it had been placed an enormous stone device in the shape of bulls' horns. The Minoans, she had been told, worshipped an earth goddess and horn symbols were part of her regalia; certainly the bull theme was fully represented in Minoan decoration, from the famous fresco of the bull-dancers to the rows of horns on the eaves of shrines.

She was tired, for Damon had been an indefatigable guide, dragging her up staircases and along corridors, and meticulously pointing out every object of interest, including the vast jars for storing oil and grain, and the tinted frescoes in the throne room, copies of the precious originals, the dark red tapered pillars. That portion of the palace had been restored, and so had the small throne itself. That would indicate, as was generally accepted, that the Minoans were a small race, a delicate, sensitive people who understand the art of gracious living. Their plumbing and drainage systems had been in advance of many modern places today. There were no fortifications, for the Minoans had relied upon their navy to protect them; they had been a great maritime power, nor had they built any great temples, and they worshipped the Earth Mother in small chapels or in grottoes on the hillsides. All this Damon had told her, and she had sensed a certain maliciousness in his thoroughness. She had accepted him in place of an official guide and he was showing her that he was conscientiously doing his duty. Finally, on their return to the central court, she had declared that she must sit down and had subsided on to the nearest stone. He was standing looking towards Mount Jouctas, on the peak of which he said there was a sacred cave which had been dedicated to the goddess. His silk knitted vest and shorts showed his slim athletic figure to advantage against a background of greenery, very different from the men of the frescoes with their gauzy kilts, wasp waists and almond eyes.

Feeling her gaze upon him, he turned his head.

'If you're not too exhausted we might visit some of the other sites. Phaestos is very attractive, there's a famous stairway ...'

'Ah, no!' She held up a protesting hand, shrinking from the prospect of climbing any more stone steps. 'It's too hot. I suppose you're used to a lot of sun, but I'm not.'

He came and sat down beside her. Though there were other people roaming the ruins, some from their ship, he had been adroit at avoiding them, and at that moment they were alone.

'It can be quite cold in Athens in the winter,' he observed.

'You live there?'

'For most of the year.'

'And do you live alone?' she questioned.

'No, with my mother.'

At last she was gaining some information about him. She asked almost timidly, for she feared he might become uncommunicative, 'Your mother is a widow?'

'My father doesn't live with us.'

A broken home? Perhaps that accounted for the cynicism she occasionally detected in him and had given him an aversion to marriage, though regarding his status in that direction she was unsure. With uncanny perception he guessed her thought.

'No, I've never been married,' he told her. 'My mother

insists that it's time I did. She wants grandchildren and I'm her only son.' He picked up a pebble and shied it at a bunch of thistles. 'What have we to offer the next generation? We haven't advanced much further than the poor wretches who perished here. The threat of a world war or another cosmic disaster hangs over our heads.'

'You're a pessimist,' Audrey said reprovingly. She had heard that point argued before. 'But life must go on——' He threw her a quizzical glance. 'Obviously the Minoans enjoyed life very much in spite of a few earthquakes. What finally wiped them out?'

'Apparently a cataclysm on an unprecedented scale. There's a theory that when the volcano at Santorini blew its top and destroyed most of that island it created such a disturbance that the backlash reached Crete, including huge tidal waves. That, it's now suggested, was the origin of the Atlantis myth. Santorini was Atlantis.'

'Now you mention it I had read something about it, but I didn't connect it with Knossos.'

He slanted a derisive glance at her. 'Knowledgeable little girl, aren't you, Audrey?'

'My father has always been interested in that sort of thing, and I suppose I've inherited a taste for it.'

'More so than discothèques and bingo?' There was a definite sneer in his voice.

'One likes to use one's brain occasionally.'

'If you've got one, most women haven't. Nor are brains much use to them if they have. Women's place is in the home.' He threw another pebble.

'Running a home needs intelligence to do it properly,' Audrey pointed out, refusing to be ruffled. 'But I'm afraid you're a reactionary, Damon. Women are no longer content with kitchen, church and children, they're demanding equality with men and proving they can get it too.'

'Perhaps that's really why I haven't married,' he observed. 'But do you really want to go out into the rat race and compete with men? Take over your father's job, push me out of mine?'

'I don't know what you do,' she hedged.

He laughed. 'Something I'm sure you couldn't.'

'Probably, but as I said before, I'm not ambitious, nor particularly bright. If I had a home and family I should regard it as a full time job. I'd only go out to work if I had to subscribe to the family budget.'

'I can provide for my wife adequately.'

'Then she'll be fortunate.'

'You think so?' He looked at her reflectively. 'You might suit me very well.'

She laughed a little forcedly. He was joking, of course, but she didn't appreciate the turn his humour had taken. It occurred to her with the force of a blow that she would very much like to be Damon's wife.

'Well, of course, if you're looking for a domesticated type,' she said lightly, 'I can cook and clean, but isn't there rather more to marriage than housekeeping?'

'Quite a bit more.' His eyes gleamed wickedly. 'Especially if you want children.'

She stood up. 'There must be quite a lot of girls of your own nationality who could fulfil your requirements,' she said coldly, 'since you're so easily satisfied.'

'But I'm not.' He looked up at her with lazy audacity. 'I would want my wife to be decorative as well as house-trained, and I also have a fancy for fair hair. Most of my countrywomen are brunettes.'

Daphne Remington-Smythe had blonde hair and was more than decorative, but she might not be domesticated. Audrey said bluntly, 'Isn't Daphne available?'

A shutter seemed to fall over his face and he turned his head away.

'I can't discuss her with you,' he said shortly.

She was was not a relative or he would have said so; the difficulty must be that she wasn't free, and that

69

accounted for Damon's continued bachelor status. It seemed obvious from his reaction to her name that she meant something to him. Audrey sighed. 'Since we've done Knossos, could we go back to the ship?' she asked plaintively. 'The sun's very hot and I'm thirsty.'

It was neither heat nor thirst that had prompted her request, but a dawning recognition that she was falling in love with this dark magnetic Greek, and her emotion was not the lighthearted experience she had imagined. His bantering talk was subtly wounding, for naturally he was only teasing, he had no serious intention towards her whatever and the mere mention of Daphne's name sent him miles away from her.

He sprang up, full of contrition. 'You poor child, you need some lunch. What am I thinking about, keeping you sitting in the sun while I ramble on about vague eventualities? Come, let's go to the car.'

That was all marriage was to him, a vague eventuality since he couldn't apparently wed Daphne Remington-Smythe.

The most outstanding feature at Heraklion was the great Venetian fort that divided the old harbour from the new. There were other signs of Venetian occupation, including an ornate fountain. For the rest it was very much a modern town with huge blocks of flats and hotels, as were to be found in most tourist centres. Damon took Audrey to lunch at a taverna where they could sit on the pavement and watch the passers-by.

There were bearded priests in soutanes and chimney-pot hats, Greek girls and boys dressed much as their British counterparts, with dark good looks that reminded her of the men on the ship. There were also many tourists of varying nationalities. Damon avoided personal topics, and discussed the Theseus legend which was so connected with Crete. Modern finds suggested that there had been no Minotaur, no labyrinth, but that

70

he went with the levy of boys and girls that were recruited to partake in the bull dances.

'So many legends are proving to have had their roots in history,' Damon remarked, 'like the story of Troy. Until Schliemann excavated the site, it was believed to be a myth.'

It was a subject that interested Audrey. Her eyes brightened and a lovely colour crept into her cheeks. Animation became her and she lost all self-consciousness, and Damon watched her with appreciation. If the discussion of ancient history could cause her to glow with beauty, how she would bloom when she was in love. She was saying:

'Theseus seems to have been a bit of a heel to have deserted Ariadne after she had helped him to escape, but I read a story in which it was suggested that she revolted him by her behaviour in the Dionysian rites.'

'More than probable—she was the priestess of a cult that indulged in some rather unpleasant practices. He has my sympathy. Dedicated women can be the very devil. She wouldn't have made a cosy wife with an eye to his creature comforts, she'd be more likely to destroy him in one of her Bacchanalian frenzies.'

'Well, she wasn't civilised,' Audrey remarked.

'From the culture you've seen today you can't call the Minoans uncivilised—and women still seek to destroy men, though they don't actually use their teeth and nails.'

He spoke so savagely that she looked at him askance. Was he speaking generally, or had he some particular woman in mind? To make him elucidate, she said:

'You've implied that poor Cheryl is a man-eater, but she's really quite harmless, all she wants is to attract a little love and admiration.'

'I wasn't thinking of your friend, she's too obvious to be a menace,' he returned. He leaned across the table and cupped her face in his hands, staring intently into her wide-spaced grey eyes. 'You'd always be loyal and true, wouldn't you, Audrey? There's no guile behind your simplicity. You've lovely eyes, like a clear stream. A man could always trust you.'

'I . . . hope so,' she faltered, unable to look away from his magnetic gaze. Such dark liquid eyes he had, and she could see herself reflected in their depths; as if she were drowning, she thought extravagantly, her personality absorbed into his. Afraid that they were attracting attention, she put her hands on his wrists and gently drew his fingers away from her face. 'Why all the drama, Damon? Has someone let you down?'

He didn't answer, and his unseeing gaze went to the passing crowd. She sensed some frustration and wondered what it could be. But he had praised her, though he had not paid her the sort of compliments she wanted to hear, he made her sound too much like a girl guide or some such worthy creature. She said impishly:

'You're being a bit deflating. I've always wanted to be a seductress.'

At which confession he burst out laughing and she looked at him reproachfully. 'Is it so impossible?'

'You could never be other than you are,' he assured her, 'a sweet, honest girl.' His face darkened. 'I only wish I were like you.'

'But that's absurd,' she declared. 'By the time I'm your age I expect I'll be . . .' She broke off. She had been going to say as disillusioned as you are, but it occurred to her that to become so, she would need an experience of men and life that she was unlikely to get. 'More sophisticated,' she amended.

'Not you. You'll settle to be an exemplary wife and mother . . . and put on weight,' he said roughly, as if his prophecy displeased him.

'How dreary!' She played with the stem of her wine-glass which was still full of the ouzo which he had per-

suaded her to sample. True to her boast of trying everything once, she had accepted it and found it nasty. 'But
to marry I'll have to fall in love,' she went on, watching
him out of the corner of her eye, 'I haven't been in love
... yet.'

'Love's not essential if your husband is a suitable person,' he told her. And he was most unsuitable, they were
poles apart by reason of nationality, circumstances and
Daphne.

'But if you want to experience the tender passion,' he
went on with a mischievous gleam in his eyes, 'without
going too far, of course, you could start by falling in love
with me.'

The brilliant colour that suffused her face at this
audacious suggestion was, she felt sure, a complete give-
away. Striving to cover her confusion, she said icily:

'That's the last thing I'd want to do.'

A little triumphant smile touched his lips and she was
sure that he did not believe her.

'It isn't a thing that can be controlled by inclination,'
he warned her. 'It can catch you unawares, and before
you know where you are, you're in the toils without hope
of escape. Poets say it's a wonderful feeling, but I've
rather forgotten what first love is like.' He dropped his
light manner and his face became sombre. 'It's much less
amusing in middle life.'

Audrey thought that was an odd choice of a word. She
didn't see how falling in love could ever be amusing, but
apparently it was to one who took it flippantly. If she
couldn't conquer her own feeling it might become a
torment, nor was she helping herself by accepting his
company and indulging in these strange half bitter, half
sweet conversations. Dimly she divined undercurrents
beneath his words which always seemed to come back
to the same subject—marriage, and she always reached
the same conclusion; he wanted to marry Daphne, and

for some reason not divulged there was a barrier.

'If I want to experiment, I'll try with Jimmy,' she observed, hoping to provoke him. 'I feel he's safer.'

'That would be unworthy of you,' he said gravely. 'The boy is young enough to be badly hurt.'

'There couldn't be any serious developments in a fortnight,' she countered.

'The damage can be done in half a day, or even half an hour.'

'I don't believe that.'

But from the first moment when she had sighted Damon on deck she had been aware of his disturbing influence. She hadn't recognised then what it portended, but she knew now.

'I assure you it's so,' Damon insisted. 'Come off it, Audrey, you know you don't care a drachma about that silly boy.'

'But I do, he's nice.'

'You seem to have said that before. If you have his welfare at heart, choke him off before he becomes too seriously involved.' His eyes suddenly narrowed and his expression was almost hostile as he added, 'Or do you find his attentions necessary to you to feed your feminine vanity?'

'What a horrid thing to say!' she cried. 'I don't need anybody's attentions, and you've done your best to destroy any little vanity I might have.'

He looked astonished. 'I've paid you several compliments.'

'Perhaps you think so, but they weren't the sort I want to hear. As for Jimmy, he knows it's only a holiday friendship like . . . like ours.'

'Not in the least like ours,' he corrected her, 'and well you know it. Be your honest self and admit . . .'

But she was stung past bearing.

'I'm sick of being called honest, loyal and good,' she

interrupted. 'Sounds like a Sunday schoolmarm. I want to be ...' She paused, for not to him could she confess her secret yearning to be a sex symbol.

Again he laughed with genuine amusement. 'You can't go against your nature, Audrey. You wouldn't be a success as a modern Delilah.'

Her moment of rebellion evaporated and she sighed. 'You're quite right, of course. I'm afraid I'll be a nice girl to my dying day. Now as we've finished lunch, will you take me back to the ship?'

'You don't want to come to Phaestos? I've hired the car for the day.'

'No, thank you, but don't waste the car, there must be heaps of girls who'd be delighted to go with you.' She had a vague idea of enhancing her own dignity by thus proclaiming her indifference.

'You're being childish,' he reproved her, completely unimpressed. Then, noticing that she had gone very pale, he added gently : 'I can see you're tired. I walked you too far this morning. Come, I'll take you back on board.'

The *Andromeda*'s next port of call was Rhodes, but though Audrey threw wistful glances in Damon's direction, he did not suggest taking her ashore there. She saw him frequently, it was difficult to overlook his distinguished figure, but he was either escorting Daphne or playing some game; he excelled at deck tennis, quoits and bridge. If he noticed her he would smile and make some casual remark, but he never tried to speak to her alone. She decided that he had tested her and found her too dull and ordinary to be interesting. But she was conscious of his speculative gaze following her whenever she crossed his vision, and Daphne watched her too. It was possible that Daphne had marked Damon's attentions to her and was taking steps to prevent her property from straying, which was a more flattering explanation of his neglect than the first idea, though the net result was the same; he was avoiding her. Daphne appeared each night in a different dress, haute couture models Audrey was sure, and put on to delight Damon's critical eye, but she held herself aloof from the other passengers, who ceased to speak to her. They described her as snobbish, stuck up and a blight upon the camaraderie of the cruise.

Rhodes proved to be an island of luxuriant vegetation, even broad-leaved banana plants flourished there. The modern town was reminiscent of the Riviera, or so Mrs Archer, who had visited it before, declared, but the huge fortress of the Knights of St John brooded over it; in fact there were few Greek remains, the old town was stamped with the seal of the mediaeval knights who had dominated it for so long.

But Audrey did not go ashore at all. She was smitten by a headache and internal upset not uncommon in the Mediterranean area, and as the day was very hot she decided to content herself with viewing Rhodes from the deck, although she was disappointed. But not half as disappointed as she would have been had she had a rendezvous with Damon.

Cheryl said she was wise, and that she had probably overdone herself trailing round Knossos in the heat, which she considered an idiotic proceeding. Jimmy half-heartedly offered to stay with her, but she firmly insisted that he must not deprive himself on her account and she would be glad of a quiet day on her own. Nevertheless she felt depressed as she watched the passengers disembarking, and the sight of Damon and Daphne strolling away together did not raise her spirits. Their elegant figures were easily identifiable from the deck.

From Rhodes the *Andromeda* turned north and the weather became slightly cooler. Recovered from her indisposition and ashamed of her low spirits, for after all she was being foolish to allow her fancy for an almost unknown man to spoil this unique holiday, Audrey enthusiastically immersed herself in preparing a fancy dress for the parade that had been inaugurated for the evening at sea. The cruise management provided a variety of entertainments for their clients, and this was one they could help to contribute towards themselves. Audrey wanted to create something original and outstanding, refusing to admit even to herself that her object was to impress Damon. She had bought a figurine in Heraklion, a replica of the Cretan priestess which she would endeavour to copy, and she would call herself Ariadne. That lady was associated with the sensual wine god Dionysus and should be able to dispel Damon's notions of her simple guilelessness, which still rankled.

The costumes were supposed to be concocted by the ingenuity of the wearers out of what they had to hand, and the shop supplied rolls of crêpe paper to assist them. Audrey made the flounced skirt out of layers of this material, the tight belt of tinfoil procured from the kitchens, stiffened with cardboard. For the bodice Cheryl lent her a velvet bolero, and the double apron, a ritual necessity, was achieved by the sacrifice of a woven shopping bag, also from the ship's shop, divided in half. The headdress, rather like an inverted hat-brim, was covered cardboard. She would never have been able to do all the work involved in the time available if Kathy and her cabin-mate had not become enthusiastic and given her generous help. The latter produced a black wig.

'It's only a cheap one, I don't expect I'll ever wear it again,' she said. 'Do what you like with it.'

In one detail Aurdey departed from her model. Minoan fashion exposed the bosom, but she covered hers with a white vest under the close-fitting bolero. Their pictorial representations also showed their women with white skins; Audrey experimented with a white wash composed of powder with which to disguise her sunburn.

When the evening came and she dressed herself in her creation, she was delighted with the result. She had elongated her eyes and broadened her brows with a black make-up pencil, and with the dark wig this effected a complete transformation. The face that looked back at her from her mirror was unfamiliar, even a little wicked. She had completely eliminated the look of wide-eyed innocence that she so deplored. Jimmy had made for her a pair of lifelike-looking snakes out of tinfoil, to carry one in each hand as the priestess did. Raising them and slitting her eyes, she decided that Damon would have to acknowledge she looked a siren now.

Cheryl who had concocted a vaguely oriental get-up composed mostly of diaphanous scarves that concealed very little of her, eyed her friend critically.

'You look a bit weird,' she commented frankly, 'but it's striking, and authentic. Of course you'll win the prize, especially as his high and mightiness Damon Grivas is one of the judges.'

'I'm sure he'll be scrupulously fair,' Audrey said hastily. She hadn't known that. Cheryl seemed able to pick up a good deal of inside information.

She saw him seated at a table with the other three officials elected for the task as she paraded round the room. Daphne had not deigned to compete. She sat behind the judges with a condescending smile on her beautiful lips, wearing a white dress of classic simplicity.

After the parade each contestant was interviewed by the compère who usually officiated at the evening entertainments. His comments, sometimes in poor taste, were intended to make his audience laugh. Only about twenty-five passengers had gone to the trouble of dressing up, the others preferred to be spectators.

The compère recognised Audrey's dress as Minoan.

'Audrey has gone to a lot of trouble to make it correct,' he said to the audience, 'but she hasn't gone quite far enough. The Cretan ladies' gowns were topless.' He turned to her with a lewd smile. 'Tell me, dear, isn't your stock as good as theirs?'

Audrey saw Damon's movement of distaste and wished she had not competed. Intuitively she guessed that he hated her being exposed to ribald remarks. Then she reflected that it was nothing to do with him, he was not her monitor, and she gave the compère a provocative smile. 'Better, but I reserve it for private viewing.'

'How intriguing, and what must one do to obtain one?'

She simpered, 'I'll tell you in confidence,' and pretended to whisper in his ear.

The man made a comic face, and gave vent to a gleeful exclamation which won the laughter he was angling for. Audrey knew she was behaving disgracefully, he would not have gone so far if she had not egged him on. There was something about Damon's grave displeasure that roused a demon of mischief in her. She gave the compère an impudent glance as she moved away and he pretended to slap her, saying:

'Naughty, naughty!'

Ther was more laughter as she left the floor to give place to the next comer, Kathy in a grass skirt of shredded paper, so burned by the sun that she could pass for the hula girl she was representing.

Audrey went to sit by Jimmy, who was frowning.

'Cheeky swine,' he growled.

'I did ask for it,' Audrey admitted, feeling a little ashamed of herself.

She was awarded first prize, but felt no triumph in her victory.

Later Cheryl told her, 'Extraordinary creature, your boy-friend, he was the only one who didn't vote for you.'

'He's not my boy-friend, but how on earth do you know?'

'I'm pally with the cruise manager who was one of the

judges. He told me he couldn't understand it. You were so obviously the best.'

Next morning the photographs of the fancy dress parade were on view. Going to inspect them, Audrey found Damon beside her.

'I gather you didn't like my costume,' she said, her eyes on her pictured form which she thought looked attractive. 'I went to some trouble to make it right.'

'Oh, the dress was a remarkable effort, but to lay yourself open to that moron's crude wit was disgusting.'

'But, Damon, it was only a bit of fun. I didn't like him . . .' She broke off at the sudden fire in his eyes that disconcerted her. Recovering, she said angrily : 'You're making a lot of fuss about nothing, and if you so disapproved of the proceedings, why were you one of the judges?'

'It was an obligation I had to fulfil, but I didn't expect to see you make such a vulgar exhibition of yourself,' he told her scathingly.

'Really, Damon, I'm not accountable to you for what I do and say,' she flashed.

'I thought you would have shown better taste,' he snapped.

'You would have preferred me to appear as a nun?' she inquired with dangerous sweetness.

'It would have been more seemly.'

'Oh, would it!' she cried fiercely, so that several people glanced round at her in surprise. Lowering her voice, she went on vehemently : 'But I'm not in the least like a nun, and you're being priggish and hypocritical. You're no saint.'

Leaning close to her so as not to be overheard, he gritted between his teeth, 'Come up on deck and I'll endorse that, and I can do better than that low scum you were encouraging.'

'I wasn't, and I won't go anywhere with you.' She was

80

scared by the naked ferocity in his eyes. 'You've humiliated me enough.'

'God almighty, didn't you humiliate yourself?'

'Oh, go away, don't pester me!' She was hurt by his fury at what had been no more than a mischievous impulse on her part. 'Don't come near me again.'

'So be it.' He felt her then, fighting between tears and anger. It was an absurd thing to quarrel about, a fancy dress that had earned his disapproval and a few impertinent remarks. But he was not English, and probably had old-fashioned notions about a girl's behaviour. Nor would he forgive what she had just said, and the implication that his attentions annoyed her. She had seen the last of Mr Damon Grivas.

Jimmy came up to her, having bought one of her photographs.

'Please autograph it for me,' he requested, holding out a pencil.

'Jimmy, you don't think I looked vulgar?' she inquired anxiously, peering at it.

'Vulgar? You? You looked superb, though I think I prefer you with your natural colouring. By the way, weren't those Cretan priestesses rather hot stuff? Orgies and things like that?' He stared at the photograph. 'You look as though you might get up to anything in that rig-out.'

Which was what Damon had disliked. Audrey decided that her attempt to look seductive had misfired.

She encountered him several times during the rest of the day, but upon each occasion he pretended not to see her. This hurt her. She was wise enough to suspect that all she was suffering from was an infatuation evoked by his handsome face and, when he chose, his charming manner, and she hoped it would fade when she returned to normal life. Meanwhile his indifference was painful to

81

her. If this was being in love, it was on experience she had no wish to repeat!

The *Andromeda* reached Lesbos during the night, and her passengers awoke to find her anchored off its shores. The little town facing them did not possess a harbour large enough to accommodate liners, and they were to be taken to it by tender. The island was still unspoiled, though a large swimming pool had been installed, which suggested it was trying to attract tourist traffic. Mithimna in the north was a place of narrow winding streets going up to the castle that crowned the hill above it. The Venetians and the Genoese had left ruined castles all over the Aegean islands where they had held sway before the coming of the Ottoman Turks.

Audrey spent the day with Jimmy and Kathy, rejoicing in the large pool which provided enough space for a real swim. They wandered up to the castle and bought souvenirs in the little shops, and apricots which were picked for them while they waited. They spent a pleasant, peaceful day and Audrey was able to forget her emotional problems. Soothed and comforted, she took her seat in the stern of the last boat back to the ship. It was about to push off when a figure came running towards it. The Greek sailor uttered a remonstrance, which Damon parried with a laughing comment in his language, then he scrambled abroad and dropped into the seat beside Audrey. The boat was not very full, most of the passengers having returned earlier. Jimmy and Kathy were in the prow looking for dolphins of which none had been seen, so that Audrey was practically isolated, and with Damon's advent her tranquillity was shattered like broken glass. His proximity had its usual disturbing effect upon her. But surely he couldn't ignore her at such close quarters, and hoping to heal the breach between them, she remarked, 'You ran it close.'

'Yes, and it would have been a long swim if I hadn't

82

caught the boat.' He glanced towards the *Andromeda* swinging at anchor across the dark blue water.

'Could you swim so far?'

'Of course, but I'd rather not have to attempt it at the end of the day, particularly as I've been on a long walk. There's a petrified tree that's one of the island's sights, but it's some distance to it. I gather you didn't attempt to find it?'

He spoke quite naturally as if there had been no rift between them, while his eyes slid over her with his usual appraisal. She had by now acquired a golden tan, darker than her hair which hung loose upon her shoulders, and her skimpy dress revealed most of her slender arms and legs; there was an almost elfin quality about her, as if she had caught some essence of the trees and water amidst which she had spent her day.

'No, I couldn't tear myself away from that lake or whatever it was, but I did get as far as the castle.'

'You look like a nature spirit,' he said softly, 'a dryad or a water nymph.'

Better than Ariadne, she was tempted to say, but no, better forget about that. Instead she shook back her hair and observed:

'I'm afraid I'm very untidy.'

'It becomes you.' He lightly touched her flowing hair. 'Could you bear to spend your life on a Greek island?'

A careless question to make conversation, or was there intention behind his words? She looked up to meet his close regard and saw that he was serious.

'I don't know. It's gorgeous on a day like this, but ...' she looked back at the receding island, 'it's very isolated and it might be a bit dreary in bad weather.'

'It is, but all Greece is not isolated.' He regarded her penetratingly. 'Have you ever considered living in another country beside England?'

'No. Why should I?'

'But your ties with England aren't so strong that you couldn't break them?' he queried.

She met his dark unfathomable eyes with a little flutter of her heart. 'If need be, I could,' she faltered.

There could be only one thing that would induce her to leave her home and family, but she couldn't believe that he meant that.

He turned his head away from her to gaze over the gently heaving water across which the sunset was spreading a reddish tinge ... Homer's wine-dark sea.

'I gather you haven't a very interesting job. Positions abroad offer more opportunities.'

His words were a douche of cold water, extinguishing the wild surmise that had briefly flickered. Naturally his proposition, if he were about to make one, would be something prosaic.

'I'm quite content with the one I've got,' she told him coolly. Then as he made no comment, 'Had you something in mind for me?'

'Yes, but if you're quite content you wouldn't be interested.'

'It depends what it is. I might consider it. Would it be on Lesbos?'

'No, in Athens, which you haven't seen yet.'

Then she thought she understood. He had told her that he had a widowed mother—no, not widowed, but apparently living alone. It might be that she wanted an English secretary or companion to help her with that language. That would account for his many appraising glances, his questions about her life and interests. He had been assessing her suitability for the post. He had even gone so far as to kiss her to discover if she were flighty. It also explained his annoyance with her appearance as Ariadne—that had not been in keeping with the picture of a self-effacing, modest young woman that he wished to present to his mother. At that moment she looked hardly more presentable, but that he would excuse after a long day on Lesbos, and she was not painted. She wore no make-up at all. Apparently he had recovered from his disapproval and was prepared to reconsider her.

Such employment had little appeal for Audrey. Mrs Grivas might be difficult and fractious; her husband, it seemed, had been unable to live with her, but Audrey would be residing in Damon's home town. The end of her holiday would not mean the sundering of her association with him. She would continue to see him, perhaps quite often, and that was a strong inducement.

The boat reached the gangway, a shaky flight of steel stairs clamped to the side of the ship, and the passengers started to climb out. Damon stood up.

'We'll talk of it again when you've thought about it.'

He helped her along the swaying boat, and reaching the gangway he lifted her over the thwart and on to its lowest step. As usual her nerves responded to his touch, warning her that if this position were in his vicinity she would be unwise to accept it, but Audrey was too infatuated to listen to wisdom. Separation was what she dreaded.

In reception she turned back to him as he entered the ship behind her.

'You haven't given me much to think over,' she complained, and added coaxingly, 'couldn't you tell me more now? You've made me so curious I shan't sleep.'

'You will, after all that sun and air.' He smiled tantalisingly down into her eager upturned face. 'It's too late to discuss it now. Besides, I need to marshal my persuasive powers to induce you to accept it.'

He was so bronzed, virile, infinitely attractive; she couldn't bear the thought that when the holiday was over, she would never see him again.

Recklessly she declared: 'I mightn't need much persuading.'

A shadow crossed his face. 'I daresay you wouldn't,' he said curtly, then he softened. 'At the moment we've only just become on speaking terms again, that's enough to be going on with.'

Audrey was left puzzled. He seemed to want her to take this position, whatever it was, and at the same time had snubbed her interest in it.

There was open supper that night since passengers had been returning at odd times. Some had dressed, others retained their day clothes. Audrey was in no hurry for a meal. She went up on deck and gazed back at Lesbos. The castle was floodlit and the lights of the town were strung like jewels beneath it.

'Where burning Sappho loved and sung.'

The line she had read somewhere recurred to her. It looked a haven of peace and refuge from the toil and moil of civilised life, but passion was all the stronger there for being primitive. What she felt for Damon was strong enough to lead her into any sort of folly sooner than for her to have to lose touch with him. She only hoped that the position he had in mind for her was in no way connected with Daphne Remington-Smythe.

CHAPTER FIVE

THE *Andromeda* entered the narrows of the Dardanelles wth their bare coastline and memorials to both the Allied and the Turkish dead in the Great War, and she crossed the Sea of Marmora in blue summer weather. Not since she left Venice had she encountered anything except calm sea and blue skies.

Damon twice asked Audrey to have a drink with him during this while; his manner was courteous and a little aloof. She was forgiven, but he hadn't forgotten, and he would give her no excuse to repeat her accusation of pestering her. Nor would he mention the proposed position in Athens, adroitly parrying her leading questions. There was plenty of time ahead of them, and why spoil a pleasant social hour by talking business? Audrey was rapidly working herself into a fever of suspense, and she knew he was well aware of her impatience which he refused to alleviate. The little ironic smile with which he evaded her infuriated her, but she had to endure his teasing. Nothing would be gained by a further tiff, nor did she dare offend him so that he would rescind that half-proffered hope of a further association.

She saw little of Cheryl, who was arduously pursuing one of the ship's officers, and had ascertained his off-duty hours and where he was likely to be found. She had not gone ashore at Lesbos, declaring that it wasn't worth seeing, and she wasn't going to risk drowning in the rocking tender, or if she didn't fall into the sea while embarking, the possibility of being seasick. Audrey did not miss her company. Jimmy and Kathy were mixing with a younger set who frequented the discothèque, which Audrey loathed, so she spent most of her hours afloat either lying in a deck chair on deck, enhancing her tan, or in the Perseus lounge weaving impossible daydreams in which Damon discovered that he loved her and they spent a blissful honeymoon on Lesbos.

The Sea of Marmora crossed, the land on either side began to converge upon the ship. Minute by minute details became clearer. On the one side the crowded shores of Anatolia, and on the other the outskirts of the great Byzantine city opposite to it. Now minarets pierced the skyline as the *Andromeda* approached Seraglio Point. Audrey, who had studied a map of the city, could pick out the dome of Haghia Sophia and the Sultan Ahmet's, or Blue Mosque, distinguished by having six minarets instead of the usual four. She could also discern the walls of the Topkapi Palace. Three waters meet below the city, the Sea of Marmora, the Bosphorous and the Golden Horn, all redolent of history.

Unfortunately the *Andromeda* was late on her schedule and it was already sunset when she reached her destination and lights were coming on all over the city.

As Audrey hung over the rail, full of excited wonder, Damon came to join her.

'A city rich in history,' he said to her, 'and full of contrasts. You'll find modern boulevards with blocks of flats, but in the older part, unpainted houses with latticed windows, patched up and leaning over drunkenly. Then there are mosques, palaces, markets, cemeteries, even Roman ruins all crowded together, but you won't see any odalisques—modern Miss Turkey is very fashion-conscious. Kemal Ataturk abolished the veil and the fez.'

'It's fabulous,' Audrey breathed, for she could think of no other word to describe the scene before her, as the *Andromeda* was slowly piloted to her berth. 'But we're making such a short stay here. Why, oh, why did the *Andromeda* have to be late?'

He shrugged. 'The hazards of travel. The ship's done very well up to now, but you'll be in time for the night club, which I understand is what most people want to go to, and the souvenir shops will stay open all the while we're in port.'

He spoke with contempt, well knowing that shopping was the most popular activity among the passengers.

'But I don't want to go to the night club, I want to see the city,' Audrey cried plaintively. 'But I daren't go on my own, not at night.'

'Certainly not,' he declared forcibly. 'But I came to look for you to tell you that I and the ship's lecturer are organising a walk through the town. You'll be quite safe as there'll be a number of us, but I must warn you it'll be fairly strenuous and through some not very salubrious places.'

'Oh, I'd love to come,' Audrey exclaimed eagerly. 'I'm quite a good walker and I don't fancy the night club.'

'That's settled, then. We'll leave directly after dinner.'

The *Andromeda* docked below the Galata Bridge, which was a blaze of light from end to end and carried a torrent of traffic. Illuminated ferry boats and other craft spangled the dark water with galaxies of shining gold. The movement and life all about them roused Audrey to a pitch of anticipation. Not only was she going to explore this glamorous place, but she was going with Damon.

To her relief Cheryl did not want to accompany her.

'I see no point in trailing round in the dark and possibly getting robbed. Istanbul is a dangerous city after nightfall,' she declared dramatically. 'I suppose you want to go because Damon's going. Really, the way you run after that man!'

'I don't run half as fast as you do after the Number

Two officer,' Audrey retorted good-humouredly. 'Is he going ashore?'

'He's on duty, worse luck, I'll have to make do with Beverley,' Cheryl said despondently, for she had not entirely dropped her American.

Nor did the Bretts want to go. 'What, miss the belly dancing?' Kathy cried. 'I've been looking forward to that.'

Jimmy said he didn't think a long walk would be very amusing, and if Damon was going he would monopolise Audrey.

'Not a hope,' she told him regretfully. 'He'll pal up with the lecturer.'

The lecturer had given those who were interested several illustrated talks about the places they were to visit, and she knew Damon was friendly with him. But there was always the hope that he would spare her a few words, and she was fairly certain Daphne would prefer to go to the night club. She could not imagine that elegant person trailing through Turkish slums, though for herself she did not mind slums, providing they *were* Turkish.

Wearing a plain dress with a cardigan and low-heeled slip-ons, Audrey went down the gangway with the fifty or so people who had elected to go on the expedition. They formed a respectful circle round the lecturer on the quay while he gave them a short discourse about the city. Then they clattered in his wake down a side street, through an arcade of brilliantly lit souvenir shops and out on to the Galata Bridge.

Audrey had always liked being out at night and the pulsing life of this huge historic city exhilarated her. On either side of them stretched the Golden Horn carrying its load of shining craft, its shores glittering with a myriad lights. To complete her pleasure, Damon came to her side and drew her arm through his.

'We mustn't lose you,' he said.

His action put the seal on her happiness. She had not dared to hope that he would single her out upon this adventure.

They left the main thoroughfare, and entered an area of somewhat dirty streets, ill-lit, with shuttered shops, an occasional café, and an assortment of mangy-looking cats. Damon's hold tightened, for the going was uneven.

'It'll be better soon,' he assured her.

'Oh, I don't mind; after all, this is where the ordinary working people live, not a show place. It's interesting.'

'I'm glad you think so,' he returned drily. 'Actually most of this is market.'

The aroma suggested that some of the merchandise had rotted.

The going became smoother and they started to ascend a steep slope, past old houses with grilled windows through which little Turkish boys grinned and waved to them. Then they were in the environs of the palace. The place was badly lit and they could not see much except the grim walls. Damon, Audrey discovered, was familiar with the place and pointed out to her the interesting features—the fountain in the place of execution where the executioner washed his hands, the imposing arch of the Middle Portal which was the main entrance to the palace. They came out on the summit of one of the many low hills on which Istanbul is built. There was another fountain, a Roman arch and the tall shape of the church of Saint Irene, and finally the huge squat bulk of Haghia Sophia and attendant minarets against the sky—the edifice which Mustapha Kemal, to avoid offending his countrymen and placate the Allies who demanded its return to Christianity, had tactfully turned into a museum. Unfortunately it was shut.

To Audrey there was something a little eerie about this pilgrimage among unlit buildings in the dark. She wished they had been floodlit, but the Turks could not be expected to cater for a mad band of enthusiasts who chose to go sightseeing at such an awkward hour. She was grateful for Damon's supporting arm, for she could not see where the curbs began and ended, and because she was walking with him among bodies too dimly seen to be recognised they seemed to be isolated. They kept on the fringe of the phalanx surrounding the lecturer, for Damon could identify the objects they passed as well as he could.

'Pity the moon isn't up,' he remarked as they passed Haghia Sophia. She murmured a vague assent, but she preferred the warm intimate darkness.

They filed into the huge courtyard of the Mosque of Sultan Ahmet, the Blue Mosque. This building was not dark, lights showed from its interior and they halted on the steps leading up to the door. Their guide was going to see if he could win admission for them. Some discussion took place while they waited hopefully, the doorkeeper or whatever he was shaking his head, but in the end he yielded to persuasion. Their leader turned to address them again.

'You may come in, but you must leave your shoes outside and trust to luck to be able to find them again.'

A triple row of wooden shelves was provided for this purpose.

One well-dressed lady announced firmly that she would not remove hers, but finding there was no option except to stay outside, she complied. Audrey was glad that she had had the forethought to wear slip-ons. Damon carried hers with his sandals to the shelf. She was not wearing tights and she walked barefoot to the sort of canvas hood that was draped over the door. One end was raised to admit them and they tiptoed inside as unobtrusively as possible; there was something about the hushed sanctity of this huge building that overawed them.

Inside the floor was covered with thick red patterned carpet. On this they seated themselves in a semi-circle around their guide while he said his piece, Audrey modestly pulling her skirt down over her bare feet. How strange differing customs were, she thought; in Catholic churches one was expected to cover one's head, and here to uncover one's feet. The expedition was taking on the unreal quality of a dream. It seemed incredible that she was actually sitting on the floor of a Turkish mosque in the centre of Istanbul at an hour approaching midnight. Four enormous columns supported the great dome, and at the further side from the door they had entered by were prayer niches and the pulpit and many windows filled with stained glass. Blue was the predominating colour of tiles and mosaics adorning walls and pillars, and electric bulbs strung on a sort of grille above their heads enabled them to see the splendour of the place.

Had she come in the daylight at a time when visitors were normally admitted she would have been impressed, but it would have been no more than usual sightseeing. But at this late hour, the huge building with its giant columns and soaring arches, jewelled windows and ornate decorations, was full of awesome mystery and their presence seemed an intrusion. She gazed wonderingly up at the great blue dome above her head with its mosaic inlays and inscriptions from the Koran. She must be dreaming, caught up in a fantasy from the Arabian nights. Far across the floor in front of a rail several men were performing their late-night devotions. She felt a sense of trespass; this was their holy place and she an infidel. She glanced at Damon, recalling what he had said about Saint Spiridon; had he the same respect for the Faithful of Islam? She found his eyes upon her, dark and unfathomable. As clear as if he had spoken she received his message, 'It's the same God, though they give Him a different name.'

They went out quietly into the courtyard to retrieve their shoes, and even then they were silent. Not until they had left the courtyard did the more irrepressible spirits start to chatter again.

They crossed the road to what had once been the old hippodrome, now a square adorned with the snake column and two obelisks, one of which was from Egypt and had stood before the Temple of Amun-Ra three thousand years ago.

The square was not illuminated and in places it was very dark. While the lecturer drew his followers from column to column expounding their history and that of the one-time racecourse, Damon detached Audrey from the crowd. Standing behind a screen of bushes, with his eyes upon the minarets of the Blue Mosque dimly seen against the sky, he asked:

'Have you thought over what I said about living in Athens?'

Audrey felt a prick of annoyance. She had never ceased to think about it, but he had refused to discuss it.

'You didn't give me very much to think over,' she said drily. 'You refused to be more explicit.'

He laughed. 'Poor child, what a shame to arouse your curiosity and not to satisfy it! Actually I wanted to sow a seed, so to speak, and give it time to germinate before I explained my proposition.'

'That sounds fine,' she said sarcastically, 'but aren't you being a bit devious? A job's a job, take it or leave it. Is there something unusual about this one that you're so reluctant to go into details?'

'I think I said a position, not a job,' he corrected her, 'though I suppose it could be regarded as one. Your acceptance is very important to me, so that's why I hesitated.' He peered at her shadowy figure. 'I need a wife,' he said bluntly.

For a second the whole darkened scene with its occasional points of light seemed to spin round Audrey, and the great Egyptian obelisk wavered above her.

'I've wondered why you hadn't married,' she began, and then she did a double take. 'A ... wife? But that can't be the position you had in mind?'

He laughed again, seeming to find her shocked surprise amusing.

'Yes, Audrey, it is. No more nor less.'

She could not see his face, it was too dark, but from his voice he did not sound very serious. Her mind was a jumble of mixed impressions. The whole expedition had seemed unreal, the glittering lights and contrasting avenues of shadows, the magnificence of the mosque, the tall monument beside them that had seen over three thousand years of history roll by—Damon's proposal was proof that she had dreamed it all. It was the climax of a fantasy. She had thought so much about the position he was to offer her that it had taken this absurd twist in her dream. When she woke she would be in her bed aboard the *Andromeda*, with all tonight's strange happenings a fading mirage. But since it was a dream, she need not try to reason or to probe. There is no logic in dreams.

'But that's wonderful,' she murmured, 'I'd like nothing better.'

There was a short pause, then companions had moved away from them and they were alone in the semi-light. Damon seemed to be a little taken aback by her instant acceptance. Then he asked:

'No questions as to why and wherefore?'

'Only one. Do you love me, Damon?'

This time the pause was longer while he hesitated, then he said:

'I'm rather past the age of romantic love, but I find you attractive and desirable, and you've other qualities that appeal to me. I could pour out a lot of sentimental twaddle, but I believe you're an honest girl and as such you deserve an honest answer. Is that good enough?'

Later she was to ponder over his words, but at that moment she was too bemused to do anything except murmur acquiescence. He came closer, slipping his arms about her and drawing her close to him. 'You're younger than your years, and it shouldn't be difficult to teach you what will be required of you.' A slightly ominous observation that she did not heed, for her whole being was flooded with rapture as he bent his head to kiss her. 'Sweet Audrey,' he whispered against her ear. 'It's easy to make love to you.'

It was very dark in the shadow of the bushes, and the square was not illuminated, only the street lights gleamed on either side where the roads crossed it. Audrey was limp in Damon's arms, her senses drugged. It was not until he put her gently away from him that she realised there was no sign of the rest of the party.

'Oh, where are the others?'

'Gone on, but don't worry about them. We'll take a taxi back to the ship.' He drew her arm through his and walked her purposefully away to where he evidently knew they would find one.

'I would like you to leave the ship at Athens,' he told her, 'and come to stay with my mother. I want you to get to know that city, since that's where we'll live.' He paused and then said firmly: 'You must be very sure that you're prepared to accept my country as your own.'

'But of course.' Then shyly she quoted Ruth, 'Where thou lodgest I will lodge: thy people shall be my people.'

He squeezed her arm against his side. 'Very pretty, my love, but you haven't seen my lodging yet.'

'I know I shall like it, but how can I leave the ship?'

'That can be easily arranged.'

Her dream was becoming more and more fantastic. No man in his senses would make such a proposition barely a fortnight after he had met her. To expect her to leave the *Andromeda* and entrust herself to him in a strange town was outside the realms of probability. And how would his mother take it? She said anxiously:

'Will Mrs Grivas be prepared to receive me?'

'I'll send her a radio message, and she'll be delighted. She's been urging me to marry for a long time. She was afraid ...' He broke off and threw her a cautious glance. 'I believe I told you she's longing for some grand-children.'

'And of course we'll give them to her, with any luck.'

It was right and proper that he should make himself clear upon that point. She would want children—his children, though she had as yet no strong maternal feelings. Nor would they have to postpone a family as so many of her friends had to do, for financial reasons. Damon was obviously affluent.

He seemed relieved. 'That's what I hope too. So many women consider them a tie, a brake upon their pursuit of pleasure.' An acid note crept into his voice.

'You seem to have known some very selfish characters,' she remarked. 'I shouldn't want anything except our home and you.' She laid her cheek against his shoulder. 'I love you.'

It was easy to confess it there in the warm intimate dark, with her arm in his. He turned his head and lightly kissed her hair.

'I knew I'd made the right choice,' he declared triumphantly.

A cruising taxi came by and he signalled to it. It drew up beside them and the obliging driver leaped out to open the door for them. Damon told him where to go and got in beside her.

'I must buy you a ring,' he said.

'At this time of night?'

'Even at this time of night. There'll be shops open by the quay. You don't imagine any of them will shut with a cruise ship in port?'

The *Andromeda* was due to sail at one o'clock.

'I don't want ever to wake up,' Audrey said as the taxi joined the stream of traffic making for the Galata Bridge.

'But heavens, child, you're not asleep!' Damon exclaimed. He slipped his arm around her. 'You won't go back on me? You'll leave the ship at Piraeus?'

'I'll do whatever you wish, Damon.'

'That's a good start,' he mocked her gently. 'Keep it up after we're married and you'll be an ideal wife.'

It thrilled her to hear him speak of her as his wife, and being married. He would never have done so in her waking life. That proved she was still dreaming. The brilliant lights on the bridge flickered into the cab and she could see his dark face inclined towards her, feel the close pressure of his arm. She lifted her hand and touched his long silky eyelashes with the tips of her fingers.

'I've so often wanted to do that,' she sighed.

'Silly little one, is that all? There are many things I want to do to you.'

Her blood stirred. 'Oh, Damon, if only this were real!'

'But it *is* real.'

The taxi had reached the quay and stopped. Reluctantly they got out and he paid the man. There were, as he had said there would be, shops still open with masses of souvenirs for sale of all prices; Turkish delight, onyx vases and jewellery.

Audrey's enchanted evening was becoming more and more extravagant. Glittering strings of beads and necklaces hanging from wires shimmered before her like an iridescent veil. Amber, jade and semi-precious stones were heaped on the counter. Damon was conversing with a stout personage with an oriental type of countenance; they seemed to know each other. Presently the man threw back the counter flap and ushered them into a small inner room lined with shelves upon which more valuable articles were displayed, an Aladdin's cave—and Damon was the magician who had created this phantasm. She was unaware of his low-voiced bargaining as she gazed about her at silver, gold and precious stones. His desire to buy her a ring was all part of the bizarre proceedings of this magic night. Surely no sane person bought engagement rings at midnight in a foreign port? Damon took her left hand and fitted a circle of brilliants on to her third finger.

'You wear it on that hand in England, I think,' he observed as he moved her hand to and fro so that the light sparkled on the gems. 'Do you like that one?'

'It's lovely,' she murmured. At that moment she would have said the same if it had been a ring from Woolworths; it was his gift and that made it unique.

Damon took out his cheque-book and the vendor led him to a small desk in one corner. As Audrey had noticed, his customer was not unknown to him; it was not the first time he had bought jewels from him for a woman. While Damon wrote he eyed Audrey critically. She was young and tender but too thin for oriental taste, but no doubt she would fatten up during a life of ease and under the experienced caresses of her lover. The Greek by repute was well versed in amorous art. Though Greek and Turk are hereditary enemies, the shopman never allowed prejudice to interfere with business, and his client was a man of means.

He murmured something in a foreign language.

'He's wishing you happiness and many sons,' Damon translated, hoping to see her blush. He knew many languages.

His hope was fulfilled. Audrey did blush, a delicate rose mounting to her cheeks, and with her luminous grey eyes shining she looked beautiful. But she was not really embarrassed; it was only a dream.

'Thank you,' she said, smiling at the vendor.

Giving her a sly look, he took a key from his pocket and unlocked a cupboard in the wall. From it he extracted a leather case and opened it. Displayed on blue velvet was a diamond pendant in the shape of a star, a lovely scintillating thing. She exclaimed in admiration and the vendor smiled, willing her to ask for it. Few women could resist diamonds and men in love were good spenders. He murmured something about a special offer.

'Do you want it?' Damon asked her.

She shook her head. 'You've spent enough for one night.'

In guttural English the man said: 'Madame will be the good housekeeper, she has thought for her husband's purse.'

Again Audrey blushed, and Damon laughed.

'I'm a fortunate man. Goodnight, Ahmet.'

Ahmet bowed. 'God go with you,' he said gravely.

'And remain with you,' Damon responded.

Outside in the brilliantly lighted arcade he halted.

'I've left my pen behind me. Excuse me, I won't be a moment.'

He turned back into the shop. Audrey moved to a stall that was displaying articles more within her price range, debating whether she would buy a souvenir for her parents, but as she had no Turkish money she decided she would wait until she reached Athens. Her father would appreciate more something Greek, and the cheaper articles looked gaudy after the contents of Ahmet's shop.

Damon rejoined her, slipping a sealed package into his pocket.

'Did you find it?' she asked, wondering if he had decided to make another purchase.

'What? Oh yes, my pen. I've got it. I hope you didn't mind waiting. It's difficult to get away from Ahmet, he was full of congratulations.' He glanced at his watch. 'Time we were getting on board.'

They walked the short distance to the ship arm in arm.

'You're mine now,' Damon told her possessively.

In normal circumstances Audrey might have challenged that statement. Women were no longer men's chattels and Damon should realise it; moreover, she was not married to him yet. But still enveloped in the euphoria of her dream, she said meekly:

'Now and always, Damon.'

Such submissiveness seemed suitable in this city of the Turks, where in the bad old days obstreperous women were drowned in sacks off Seraglio Point, as Damon proceeded to tell her. She shivered.

'Ugh, how gruesome, but you're not a Turk.'

'I can be jealous,' he warned her.

She preceded him up the gangway into the ship. Although it was past midnight the decks were still thronged with people waiting to see the last of this glamorous port that they had only been able to visit so briefly, when the *Andromeda* slipped her moorings. Lights still blazed on either side of the Galata Bridge and across the water in Anatolia, their reflections rippling the dark sea with gold.

The bar on the after-deck was open and Damon insisted that Audrey must have a drink, but he made a face when she asked for orangeade.

'Poor stuff in which to celebrate a night like this.'

'I'm thirsty,' she said simply.

She sat beside the pool while he fetched it for her. The ship was dressed overall with coloured light bulbs which also outlined the stern. Pleasantly tired, Audrey sat gaz-

101

ing at them and did not notice that Damon was rather a long time.

He returned at last and with him came Daphne Remington-Smythe, dressed in a long blue gown glittering with silver trimming, and about her neck was a diamond star very similar to the one the Turk had shown to Damon.

Now surely Audrey had reached the climax of her dream's inconsequence, for instead of looking displeased or put out, Daphne was smiling in a friendly fashion; her blue eyes were kind and she said pleasantly: 'I hear I have to congratulate you, Audrey.'

Audrey murmured her thanks. Daphne had never called her by her name before. She drank her iced orangeade thirstily, and Damon and Daphne had whisky. She did not notice the meaning glance that passed between them over her head.

The ship's siren sounded and slowly she began to move. They went to the side to see the last of the glittering panorama of Istanbul slide by.

'I don't want this night ever to end,' Audrey said happily.

Damon looked at his watch. 'It has ended, it's after one o'clock. Time you went to bed, little one.' There was dismissal in his tone.

They walked with her to the head of the stairs leading down to her cabin. She was disappointed, she had hoped for a goodnight kiss from Damon, but all he did was touch her fingers with his lips as she held out her hand to him. He would not embrace her with Daphne present.

She looked back when she was half-way down. They made a striking pair as they stood side by side watching her. She was so fair, he so dark, and she nearly as tall as he, her silken gown clinging to her well-rounded figure, which made Audrey's slenderness look childish. He as usual looked elegant. He had that undefinable attribute called style; even in rags he would have looked distinguished, but his well-cut beige jacket, silk shirt and light trousers could not be faulted. He looked remote, as if the dream sequence was beginning to fade and their relationship to fall back into normal perspective, as it had been before she had gone ashore ... if she had gone ashore. Was it possible that she had never left the ship? She raised her hand in salutation to the two above her before resuming her downward journey when the angle of the stairs would take her from their sight. Damon's face was inscrutable, but Audrey saw with faint discomfort that Daphne's expression was one of pity.

Cheryl was in bed and asleep when she entered their cabin. She was glad of that, she did not want to face questions, or as was more likely, have to listen to an account of her friend's trivial doings. Fatigue had overtaken her, she had walked a considerable distance and experienced a welter of emotions. Or had she? The events of the evening were already fading into a mist of unreality. Too tired to question further, she stripped off her clothes and tumbled into bed without bothering to wash or cream her face and instantly fell into the deep sleep of exhaustion, lulled by the familiar slight motion of the ship and the distant throb of her engines. The last lights from the coast were merged in distance as the *Andromeda* passed into the Sea of Marmora on her way to Athens and whatever fate held in store for Audrey there, but she was too dead asleep even to dream.

She awoke quite late to the steward's knock and found Cheryl fully dressed, regarding her curiously.

'I ordered breakfast for you as you seemed dead to the world,' she explained as the man brought in a tray.

'*Kalimera*, madame,' he said, and silently withdrew.

'God, you look a mess,' Cheryl went on. 'That crazy

103

walk was too much for you. You should have come with us. The night club was super.'

She chatted on while Audrey regarded her sleepily, trying to collect her muddled thoughts. What had she done last night? Fallen asleep in the lounge after dinner and dreamed an impossible dream?

Suddenly Cheryl stopped in mid-sentence and swooped forward, seizing Audrey's left hand.

'Where on earth did you get that?'

Audrey stared blankly at the circle of brilliants sparkling in the morning light, and looked up into Cheryl's startled face.

'A . . . a souvenir,' she faltered.

'Come off it, that ring's a good one, and on that finger! Seems you've got yourself a man, unless you were drunk. Tell me all about it.'

'I . . . I can't remember.' Audrey twisted the ring, trying to disentangle her chaotic recollections. So it hadn't been a dream, but what had she done? To what had she committed herself?

'Then you must have been drunk. Eat your breakfast and when I've had mine, I'll come back and we'll try and sort out what folly you've let yourself in for. It's always you quiet unobtrusive girls who get into trouble.'

With which parting shot Cheryl left the cabin.

Audrey reached for the coffee pot and poured out a full cup; she needed it.

Damon—had he really proposed and she had accepted him? The ring seemed to be confirmation of that. But now the doubts and questions came thick and fast. Why had he been so precipitate? Had they both been carried away by an overwhelming passion that had resulted in her promise to leave the ship at Athens? What would her parents say? Would Mrs Grivas really be pleased to receive her? Most important of all, did Damon really love her?

She was not so infatuated that she did not realise the enormous risks they would be taking, for they knew very little about each other and nothing at all of their respective backgrounds. A crazy teenager might have urged an immediate union, looking no further ahead than sexual gratification, but Damon was too mature to yield to such impulses. With his cynical attitude towards matrimony she would have expected long and cautious deliberation before he made an irrevocable decision. If it were irrevocable.

Cheryl's suggestion recurred to Audrey. Had *he* been drunk when he bought the ring for her, though he had shown no signs of it? Was he this morning regretting his rash action? She did not herself repent of anything that had happened. If Damon were prepared to take a chance on her, she was more than ready to take one on him, but she needed his reassurance that he had meant all he had said.

There was only one way to ascertain that. She must see him, talk to him in the broad light of day when they were no longer influenced by the sensuous magic of the Byzantine night.

CHAPTER SIX

AUDREY found Damon playing deck tennis on the upper deck. Normally she would have watched with pleasure, as his lithe muscular figure in singlet and shorts showed to advantage in the energy of the exercise, but this morning she was impatient to speak to him and longed only for the game to end. She was not pleased to see Daphne among the onlookers, affectedly applauding every time Damon won a point. She was at the opposite side of the deck to Audrey and either did not or pretended not to see her. Damon noticed her, for he waved to her, but he did not break off his game as she had half-hoped he would. The four young men were fairly equally matched and it looked like going on for some time.

The upper deck caught the breeze and soon Audrey's hair was blown into a hopeless tangle. Daphne was wearing a bandeau to keep hers in place and her trim slacks and top were more suited to the weather than Audrey's thin dress, which threatened to blow over her head at any moment. Her immaculate appearance was a further annoyance to Audrey, whose spirits were sinking lower and lower. From time to time she glanced at the ring on her finger to give herself confidence. That was real and proof that the events of the previous night had actually happened.

At last the game finished. Flushed and excited, for he and his partner had won, Damon went to speak to Daphne, who congratulated him fulsomely, and then came across to Audrey.

'Good morning, little one. Your friend told me you

weren't up, as you were laid out by your exertions last night. How do you feel now?'

'Fine,' she murmured mechanically, then with more energy, 'Damon, we must talk. Can we go somewhere private?'

'Dear me, that sounds ominous, and privacy is hard to find on this ship.'

He wasn't taking her plea seriously, but surely he must realise she was anxious to discuss the practical side of their situation? 'There's my cabin,' she suggested. She had never located his.

'With the steward likely to butt in at any moment and think bad thoughts?' His tone was gently mocking. 'Besides, at this time they're usually cleaning the cabins. We might try the Perseus Lounge, most people are out on deck.' He indicated that she should precede him. 'What about a mid-morning drink?'

The usual formula. 'I wouldn't mind a coffee,' she told him.

'We'll collect one en route, and I could do with a beer after all that exercise.'

The cruise manager waylaid him at the bar, so Audrey took her cup and went into the lounge to wait for him. She wondered if he were purposely delaying their conversation, or was her uncertainty causing her to be hypersensitive? She hoped Daphne would not take it into her head to follow them.

He came at last, carrying a half-consumed glass of beer.

'Sorry about that,' he apologised. 'A small problem. What did you want to talk about?'

'Us,' she replied promptly. 'You did mean all you said last night?'

He looked startled. 'Good God, girl, of course I did. I thought it was all settled. You'll disembark at Piraeus and I'll take you to my mother's house in Athens.'

Nervously she twisted the ring on her finger. She had been too carried away to think clearly, but now in the bright daylight this precipitate plan of his seemed preposterous.

'I don't think I can do that, Damon. I want to go home first and see my parents. They ... they'll be so surprised.'

And probably, she judged, concerned.

A flash of irritation crossed his face, but he spoke gently.

'Don't you see, it's so convenient. You'll be right on our doorstep, so to speak. You can break your journey with us and go home afterwards if you so wish.' He shot her a keen glance. 'Do you expect opposition from your family?'

'No, not exactly.' She sounded doubtful. 'But naturally they'll want to know all about you.'

'They can find out anything they want to know from Matthew Gregory. He's a great friend of your father's, isn't he?'

'Uncle Matt?' She was surprised. 'Oh yes, he's my godfather.'

'I knew that, and quite a lot of things about you before we actually met. He gave you quite a testimonial. It seems he thoroughly approves of you, and as he approves of very few people you ought to be flattered.'

She was still more astonished, for though she had known Matthew all her life he had usually ignored her. 'He ... he's never taken much notice of me.'

'He sees a lot without appearing to notice.'

'But what's your connection with him?' she asked with faint bewilderment. 'You seem to know him well ... I suppose you've met over business? You're both interested in shipping?'

She looked at him interrogatively. She did not know exactly what his business was, and it was time he became more explicit.

'We are, and shipping can be very profitable if you know your way about. I was born to it, so to speak.' He drained his glass then said deliberately: 'Matthew Gregory is my father.'

'Your father?' She stared at him. So the resemblance had not been her fancy. She could see it clearly now—those magnificent eyes, Matthew's one good point, the arrogant set of the head.

'Yes. He anglicised our name, turning Grivas into Gregory after my mother left him, and of course he's British. Said it was better for business. Actually I had to choose my nationality when I was twenty-one as I was born in England, but I prefer to be Greek, like my mama. The trouble was that she couldn't stick England, and he didn't want to live in Greece. She said England was so cold, and she didn't mean only the climate. She missed her own people. We Greeks rather tend to cling to our families.'

'Then why do you want to marry me?' Audrey exclaimed, dismayed by these revelations. 'I'm English. Suppose I don't like Greece?'

'That's what we have to find out, and the sooner the better. It's for that reason I want you to stay in Athens.'

'Yes, but ...' He frowned and she realised she had used the word he disliked. 'It's all happened so suddenly,' she went on, pushing her hair off her forehead. 'And now you tell me you're Uncle Matt's son. I knew vaguely that he had one, of course, but he ... I mean, you never seemed to come to England. I can't take it all in.'

'You'll soon get used to the situation,' he assured her. 'Women are very adaptable.'

'Apparently your mother wasn't—she wouldn't stay in England.'

He smiled. 'We have more sunshine than you do.'

She did not think that was a very pertinent explanation, though a Greek might come to hanker for blue

109

skies during a grey northern winter. A sudden suspicion darted into her mind.

'Was this Uncle Matt's idea?'

He was engaged in lighting a cigarette and he did not look at her.

'He approves,' he told her. 'He sent you on this cruise so that we could get to know each other. He'd arranged I'd be on this ship doing a sort of market research. He has shares in the company and wants a report on the way it's run.'

So that had been Matthew Gregory's motive in offering her this holiday! Audrey recalled all Damon's appraising glances that had been so like the way Matthew had looked at her that day in his office. He had been sizing her up, comparing the reality with the description his father had given of her. She remembered something else; her own father had told her that in Greece godfathers expected to have a hand in arranging their godchildren's marriages. Matthew had selected her as a suitable mate for his son and had sent her to meet him to be accepted or rejected, in other words, on approval.

'Did you plan all this before you met me?' she asked in a choked voice. 'Is Uncle Matt making it worth your while?'

His eyes flashed. 'Certainly not! I'm quite capable of choosing my own wife and supporting her, though naturally I've expectations from my father, and it's satisfactory to know that he'll approve of my choice.'

'Oh, very, if it *is* your choice and not his!'

His hand shot out and gripped her wrist as it lay on the table.

'Don't dare to say things like that or I'll have to punish you.'

She tried to free her wrist, her eyes sparkling irefully.

'You'll not intimidate me with stupid threats! I hate to think I've been bartered.'

110

'Don't be melodramatic.' He threw her wrist away, and a glint of appreciation come into his eyes. 'I'm pleased to see you've spirit. I don't care for meek little mice.'

'Are you sure you care for me at all?'

He sat back in his chair and laughed. 'The eternal feminine question, except that its usual form is *do you love me*? Audrey, Audrey, do you realise we're nearly quarrelling? And over what? The fact that my father knew you first and thought you would make me a good wife? Well, I'm in full agreement with him for once— we don't always see eye to eye, providing . . .' voice and mien became serious, 'you decide you can bear to live in Greece. As I said, that's why I want you to come home with me when we reach Athens, to get the feel of the place. If you like it . . . splendid. If you don't, and I hope to God you will, we mustn't risk another split-up like my parents', for I couldn't make my home in England even for you; in fact for material reasons it's impossible.'

'I wouldn't expect you to do that,' she said earnestly. 'A wife's place is with her husband.' Then fearing that that sounded like criticism of his mother, she added hurriedly, 'except in exceptional cases. But couldn't I come out later on?'

'I see no point in delaying your visit. I want to show you my home town, now, at once. I believe you'll love it.' His eyes began to glow with enthusiasm. 'You feel for old things, and there are so many monuments that will appeal to you. Beautiful relics of a glorious past. Delphi, for instance, will fire your romantic imagination, and those great crumbling ruins below Parnassus. Weren't you excited by the past civilisation of Crete? Didn't you thrill to the atmosphere of the Blue Mosque? Moreover, in the intimacy of cruise life I've come to know a lot amout your character. You've a very charming person-ality, my little nymph.'

His voice dropped to a low note, subtly caressing, and Audrey melted.

'I'm sure I'll love Greece,' she said, her eyes shining. 'The cruise only allows one day there, but you'll show me all of it?'

'I'll be delighted, but I do have to do some work. But there'll be the weekends.'

She looked startled. 'How long shall I stay there?'

'For always, I hope.'

She had the sensation of being swept off her feet.

'But I'll have to go home some time.' He frowned. 'I mean, I'll need clothes, and shouldn't we be married in England?'

'We can settle all those details when you've made your decision,' he said easily.

'About living in Greece?'

His eyes glowed. 'You've decided about wanting to marry me?'

'I want that more than anything in the world.'

His hand still lay upon the table and she put her cheek against it while a wave of emotion welled up in her. 'Oh, Damon!'

'Oh, Audrey!' he mimicked her. 'I don't think it will be difficult to teach you to see my country through my eyes.'

With his free hand he stroked the soft masses of her hair.

'You'll never cut this off. I forbid it.'

She thrilled to the mastery in his voice.

'Then I never will.' She looked up with a gleam of mischief in his eyes. 'Nor will I ever wear Cretan dress again. You were nasty about that, Damon.'

'I didn't like my Vestal Virgin looking like a heathen goddess,' he explained, 'nor aping the manners of an antique tart.' Audrey winced. She was ashamed of her behaviour on that night, but had not got so far as to admit it. 'You won't be a Vestal Virgin much longer, my love,' his voice deepened with a passionate note. 'It'll be sweet teaching you how to love.'

'You've done that already,' she murmured.

It was not quite what he had meant, but he said nothing and she went on: 'I'd no idea love could be so . . . so devastating. You're my whole life, Damon.'

'Charming as it is to hear you say such things, this isn't the time or the place,' he observed drily. 'I can't make the proper response, there are too many people about. But my time will come,' he added darkly, 'when I'll repay them with interest.'

As they would reach Piraeus next day the more practical aspects had to be considered. Damon told her he had sent his father a message by radio, but as regards her family she could write from Athens. The *Andromeda* had another call to make at Dubrovnik, so she would not be expected home for several days.

'And I daresay Papa Matthew will give them a hint,' he said airily. He always referred to his father by his first name, occasionally prefixed by Papa.

'They'll be surprised, they haven't any idea,' Audrey faltered in protest.

'Think not?' He gave her a quizzical look.

She disliked the implication behind those two words. Had Matthew discussed the possibility of this marriage with her father? Such collusion was a violation of her independence, but Damon would consider it right and proper. He told her then that his father frequently came to Greece, though he didn't stay at his wife's house.

'To make sure I was being properly brought up,' he explained, 'and when I was old enough, to initiate me into the business.'

Audrey was not to be diverted from the point at issue.

'Your mother won't be expecting me,' she demurred.

'Oh yes, she is. I phoned her from Istanbul.'

113

He must have done that before their memorable walk on Seraglio Point; it had been too late afterwards.

'I hadn't agreed to come then,' she objected, thinking he took far too much for granted, 'nor were we engaged.'

'Maybe I was anticipating a little,' he admitted cheerfully. 'She understood there was an element of doubt.'

But not in his mind. Audrey was certain that he had been sure of her compliance from the moment when he had mentioned a 'position' as they left Lesbos. She had a sensation of being manoeuvred which she resented, but she had gone too far to draw back, and she was being petty to question his methods since the end product, their engagement, was what they both desired.

Since she was leaving the ship at Piraeus, it was necessary to tell Cheryl of her change of plans. She had expected grumbles but to her surprise her friend seemed to be genuinely perturbed.

'He's fascinating, of course, and you've lost your head as well as your heart, but for God's sake, girl, have a little sense,' Cheryl besought her. 'Are you even certain there *is* a mother?'

Audrey pointed out that being Matthew Gregory's son was proof of his integrity.

'You've only his word for it,' Cheryl observed drily. 'And I always thought that phoney uncle of yours was a bit suspect. About the business connection I've no doubts, but the personal part is too like a fairy story. Surely if this match were hatching your parents or your godfather would have given you a clue?'

'I expect they wanted us to meet without prejudice,' Audrey declared, knowing that if she had received any such hint she would have avoided Damon. 'We might have disliked each other at sight.'

'Highly improbable. If he made up to you, you were bound to fall for him, and you've got a sort of elusive charm that probably appeals to him after the brazen advances of the hussies who run after him. Audrey love, I'm not trying to be starchy. You know I'm not conventional, and it's often a good idea to sleep with a fellow you're gone on to get him out of your system; but as for this hare-brained scheme of going with him to Athens, you've no guarantee that he won't leave you stranded when he's got what he wants. I'm fond of you, Audrey, I'd hate you to be let down, but you're not hard-boiled enough to be able to cope with a wolf like this Damon Grivas, whom I don't trust an inch.'

Audrey had half expected Cheryl to be jealous and consequently spiteful, but she could not doubt that her friend's concern was sincere and she was touched by it. She knew there was some sense in what she said, but her faith in Damon remained unshaken.

'You don't understand,' she protested. 'We love each other, and what's love without trust?' She forgot that Damon had not yet said those three magic words, 'I love you.'

Cheryl looked at her friend's face, which shone with a faint radiance. Love had transformed her into real beauty.

'You're besotted,' she said ruefully, 'and it's hopeless to argue with you. But has he explained his connection with the glamorous Daphne?'

'He's told her we're engaged and she congratulated me,' Audrey informed her triumphantly.

'How magnanimous of her!' Cheryl exclaimed. She added cryptically, 'That woman's no fool, she'll be too clever for you.'

'What do you mean?' Audrey asked uneasily.

'That I don't suppose you've seen the last of her.'

'Please,' Audrey's lips quivered. 'Don't be horrid, Cheryl, if there was anything between them it'll be over when we're married.'

'When you're married,' Cheryl said emphatically. 'And

if it does come off, you're asking for trouble. He's a foreigner, and he'll expect you to conform to all sorts of funny customs. He'll probably bully you, once the first rapture's over, besides being unfaithful ...'

'That will do, Cheryl,' Audrey cut in sharply. 'It's my risk and I'm prepared to take it. Now I must get on with my packing.'

She resolutely pushed away the faint doubts aroused by her friend's words as she filled her cases. Cheryl prided herself upon her knowledge of the world, and took a cynical view of humanity, especially male humanity, that was partly a pose. She could not understand the beautiful thing that had blossomed between herself and Damon. As for the doubt that he was Matthew's son, that was quite absurd. Not only was there that fugitive physical resemblance, but they were alike in manners. She recalled with a little tender smile their mutual objection to her frequent use of the word 'but'. There would be no buts in her future, she would leave it unquestioningly in Damon's hands and he would never fail her.

The *Andromeda* sailed into Piraeus harbour in the early afternoon, where the water was filthy and the view entrancing. On either side were the packed houses on arms of land running seawards, and behind them a backdrop of distant mountains. The quays and docks were crowded with shipping flying the flags of all nations.

There was the usual manoeuvring by tugs to push and pull the *Andromeda* into her berth. A steward came to collect Audrey's luggage. She had said goodbye to Cheryl and asked her to tell the Bretts and her other acquaintances that she had left. She did not feel equal to facing their curiosity. She went up on deck to watch the passengers disembarking, wondering where Damon was and if she was expected to go and find him, but when the first rush ashore was over a disembodied voice over the tannoy requested:

'Will Miss Winter please go to the cruise office.'

With fast-beating heart she went down to Reception. Damon was there, looking unfamiliar in formal clothes, a grey suit, light blue shirt and tie. She had put on the thin coat she had brought with her for cooler days, of which there had been none, over a flowered dress, and wore a shady hat. How respectable we look, she thought involuntarily.

Damon ran a critical eye over her apparel, seemed satisfied and took her arm.

'Our luggage has gone ashore,' he told her.

The *Andromeda* was docked beside a wide expanse of concrete opposite to the Customs offices, a low echoing building through which they had to pass to gain the street beyond, though as they were cruise passengers nobody took any notice of them.

'I shall have to get you a resident's permit,' Damon remarked as they reached the blinding sunshine of the street where a taxi awaited them. Tall buildings lined the further side of it, and along the quay side, bougainvillea had been trained like standard roses, a row of brilliantly coloured bouquets.

As she entered the taxi, Audrey glanced back at the ship in which she had made this fateful journey. The big white structure stood out against the azure sky, the blue and white flag of Greece idly flapping at her stern. There lay the last of her old life, and the taxi was carrying her through this bustling teeming city towards the unknown. For once her adventurous spirit was damped. Damon, sitting beside her, was the one familiar thing among all this strangeness, and glancing towards him she realised that he was not familiar at all. That proud profile of his was wholly Greek and this was his country, but it was not hers, and there was no going back. Was Cheryl right, and was she acting crazily by putting her future into his hands?

'The Toureolimano Yacht Basin.' He indicated a semi-circular bay on their right which they were passing. It was crowded with small ships from fishing boats to cabin cruisers, its waterfront lined with cafés, a bright gay scene in the clear sunshine.

But Audrey was not interested in the yachts, she needed reassurance. Raising her eyes to his, she murmured faintly:

'You'll be good to me, Damon? You're all I've got now.'

'Why the sudden tragedy, Audrey *mou*? Of course I'll be good to you.' His smile was indulgent, as if he spoke to a timid child. 'You're not completely cut off, you know. If you feel homesick you can ring up your parents from Athens!'

Oh, blessed speed of modern communications—this statement was more reassuring than any protestations of devotion would have been.

'But isn't it terribly expensive?' she asked.

'Expense is no object. Matthew is always ringing up. You can call them tonight if you're so inclined.'

Audrey brightened; tonight she would hear her father's voice and discover what he thought about her proposed marriage, and Damon would not have suggested it if he thought he would disapprove. Her momentary depression lifted, and she began to peer out of the window with interest.

'Syntagma Square,' Damon said. 'The centre of Athens.'

Audrey looked about her eagerly, admiring the wide streets that flanked a paved centre with trees and fountains. To one side commanding it was the classical front of the one-time Royal Palace.

'But it all looks so modern,' she complained.

'It is modern, most of Athens is, the old town was quite small.'

Lycabettus, that steep conical excrescence rising above the streets and houses, next caught her eye. It seemed to her more quaint than beautiful. They rounded a corner beside the wide space that had once been the immense temple of Zeus, of which all that remained was a cluster of tall Corinthian pillars. Then finally the Acropolis, its steep escarpment crowned with honey-coloured temples glowing in the afternoon sun.

'We're nearly home,' Damon told her.

Hermione Grivas, it transpired, lived in an old house on the road going past the Acropolis. Few of the houses still standing in that locality were still used as residences; it belonged to the period following Greek independence when buildings were erected in, oddly enough, a Victorian style which in its turn had aped the classical. It had the pillared porch so frequently seen among London houses, and large high-ceilinged rooms. Modern Greeks of means preferred the wide-balconied flats in the newer streets, but Mrs Grivas clung to the roof that had sheltered her parents and grandparents. It had been brought to Matthew as part of her dowry following the tradition that the bride provided the home. It would in the course of time be demolished to make way for a more modern erection, but meanwhile it stood below the hill that supported the remains of Athens' ancient glory.

At the time of the Turkish evacuation the capital had been a poverty-stricken town of a mere six thousand inhabitants, decaying neglected amidst its despoiled ancient ruins. Since then it had grown and spread into a huge sprawling modern city, only the Plaka district retaining its ancient charm.

The taxi stopped outside the gate of a strip of garden shaded by an acacia tree and Damon said, 'This is it.'

Audrey stood nervously looking up at the Ionic

119

columns on either side of the front door above a flight of steps while Damon paid off the taxi. A man came hurrying round from the back to attend to their luggage, hailing Damon enthusiastically in Greek. The Kyria Grivas, he said, was awaiting them in the salon. Damon ran up the steps to the front door which he threw open, beckoning to her to follow.

'Welcome, *agape mou*, to the House of the Olives, for that's its name, though I'm afraid the olive groves that once surrounded it have long since disappeared.'

'Damon, Damon, is it you, my son?' a clear high voice called in Greek, and Hermione Grivas came to greet them.

She was only of middle height and slim, though she had such immense dignity that she seemed tall. She wore a Parisian suit of dark blue and her perfectly coiffured hair was a reddish brown, obviously tinted. Her eyes were greenish hazel and shrewd. Audrey, who had expected someone dark and probably stout, was startled. She was not in the least like her son.

'*Ti karni*, Mama,' Damon bent to kiss her cheek. 'This is Audrey,' he went on, drawing the girl forward, 'Audrey Winter.'

'*Né*, Matthias has spoken of her.'

It took Audrey a couple of seconds to realise that she meant her husband.

'And I also spoke of her from Istanbul,' Damon reminded her. 'Mama, Audrey and I are to be wed.'

The arched eyebrows rose. 'You have decided?'

'Definitely.'

Mrs Grivas asked a question in Greek and Damon frowned.

'Audrey does not understand Greek.'

'Then she will have to learn it, but I am discourteous. Welcome, Thespoinis Winter, and come in out of the sun.'

She gave Audrey a tight smile which did not reach her eyes.

'Call her Audrey,' Damon protested.

'You permit?'

'I'd be glad if you would, madame.'

The 'madame' seemed to please the autocratic lady, and her smile was more friendly.

'Georgi will have taken up your baggage,' she announced, in her heavily accented English. 'You would like to go to your room, né?' She led the way to the foot of the stairs. 'Afterwards we will have the cup of tea.' She slanted an inquiring look at Damon. 'English tea.'

'Well done, Mama,' he said with a grin.

Audrey's room had a large window overlooking the wide road and the ruins of the Dionysius theatre on the further side, overshadowed by the gaunt cliff of the Acropolis. There was a stone balcony outside it shaded by a sun-blind. The furniture was characterless and might have been displayed by any British furniture shop. The bed was a low divan.

'There is the bathroom there,' Hermione Grivas indicated a further door. 'Come downstairs when you have arranged yourself and tea will be there. Now please to excuse, I have much to say to my son.'

I bet you have, Audrey thought as the door closed behind her hostess. You haven't taken to me, that's obvious. She began to wish that she hadn't come. In fairness to Hermione Grivas she had to admit it must have been something of a shock to have a totally strange young woman suddenly dumped upon her as her son's fiancée. She removed her coat, brushed her hair and washed her hands in the very ordinary small bathroom with its basin and shower. Nostalgically she thought of the *Andromeda*, still berthed in Piraeus. Why had Damon insisted upon this visit? It would have been so much pleasanter to have finished the cruise together and flown back to London, where she could introduce him to her family. He wanted her to familiarise herself with Athens before making her final decision and she supposed there was reason in that, but would she be expected to live with his mother after they were married? It was a daunting thought.

The salon, Hermione's sitting room, was at the back of the house with doors opening on to a stone verandah, its view was obstructed by the next property, from which it was divided by a row of cypresses. There was nothing Greek about its furnishings except for a few replicas of antique vases, nor were there any photographs or personal belongings visible to give a hint of Hermione's tastes.

Tea was poured out of a silver pot into delicate china cups with, inappropriately it seemed to Audrey, a pattern of rosebuds. Her grandmother had a very similar set for company use in her farmhouse and it had always struck her as being typically English. With the tea were plates of cucumber sandwiches and *petits fours*.

'So you and my son desire to wed,' Hermione said bluntly to Audrey, after a spate of polite enquiries about her journey. 'Have you considered that you will have to make the adjustments very many? If you are to be Greek wife, you will not have the same liberty as you do in England.'

'Mama, *parakalo*,' Damon intervened, 'give the girl a chance! Audrey has only just arrived. Let her absorb her first impressions in peace.'

Undeterred, Hermione went on, 'Matthias is your godfather, is he not? Your family and he are ...' she hesitated for the right word. 'Much intimate, is it not? Matthias has spoken well of you and promises to make provision.' (What on earth does she mean by that? Audrey thought.) 'So it would seem that all is as it should be when you have, as Damon say, absorbed your impressions. There is no reason for delay. The sooner you are married, Damon, the more pleased I shall be.'

That should have sounded encouraging, but somehow it did not. The look Hermione bestowed upon her son was almost menacing, and to Audrey's astonishment Damon coloured, a dull red mounting to his olive cheeks.

'That depends on Audrey,' he began, and his mother cut in swiftly.

'Zut, you will not I hope be ruled by a girl's whims? It is her part to obey your wishes.'

Audrey felt a spurt of anger.

'I don't know what you mean by whims, madame,' she said quickly, 'but I must have time to, as you say yourself, adjust. Much as I love Damon,' she blushed charmingly, 'I can't allow myself to be rushed. It ... it's a very big decision to make, and I too have parents who will expect to be consulted.'

'I thought it was all arranged,' Hermione spoke stiffly.

'How could it be in so short a time?' Audrey cried, feeling enmeshed. Had she, by coming to Damon's home, committed herself irrevocably?

Hermione's eyes narrowed spitefully.

'Procrastinate and you'll lose him,' she snapped.

'Mama, what a thing to say!' Damon expostulated.

'Forgive me,' she said meekly. 'It is that I do not understand these modern ways. When I was young a girl's parents did the matchmaking and she wedded the man provided for her. As I did.'

Damon's eyes met Audrey's with a glint of amusement. Hermione's marriage was hardly a good advertisement for the procedure she was advocating, but she seemed quite unaware of it. He put down his cup.

'What would you like to do, Audrey?' he asked. 'It's still early and we don't dine until late. Do you want to rest, or shall we climb the Acropolis? From there you can see all over Athens.'

'I'm not at all tired,' Audrey told him. 'And I'd love to climb the Acropolis.'

Anything to get out of that house which seemed to be stifling her, and away from this unsympathetic woman and her ambiguous remarks. It was strange that although she did not appear to approve of her daughter-in-law-to-be, she seemed anxious to hasten the marriage.

Mrs Grivas' eyebrows went up again and she began to expostulate, but in her own tongue.

Damon laughed.

'You're out of date, Mama—girls, even Greek girls, don't have chaperons nowadays, and we shan't be alone on the Acropolis. Too many tourists.'

And that, Audrey thought as she ran upstairs to fetch her hat, is about the limit!

With all due deference to Damon's mother, if she had to stand much more of her antediluvian nonsense, there was bound to be an explosion. Again she wished that she had not come.

Audrey's spirits revived when in the golden air of the late afternoon, she and Damon climbed the steep slope and then the steps to the place below the Propylaea where they bought their admission tickets. They passed between the huge ruined columns out on to the marble paving that had once been the Sacred Way. It was scarred and broken now. The imposing bulk of the Parthenon was before them, the graceful Erectheum with its porch of supporting caryatids to their left. Again Audrey felt awed; it was so vast and so ancient, and for centuries man had come here to worship the gods of antiquity until it was desecrated by the Turks.

They picked their way among huge blocks of fallen marble; marble was one thing in which the Greeks were rich. Past the Parthenon on the further side they looked over a wall to see, as Damon had promised, the mass of streets and houses that made up Athens reaching to the mountains that ringed the city.

Audrey asked: 'Why is your mother in such haste for us to be married?'

He laughed easily. 'She's afraid I might change my mind. She can't believe that I'm really caught.'

'Are you?' she asked provocatively.

'My love, don't dare to doubt it.'

There were not many people on that side, several expeditions had departed and new arrivals had only just reached the Proplaea. Damon's arm went round her and he pressed her to his side.

'Don't keep me waiting too long,' he murmured in her ear.

'But you said I must be sure,' she reminded him, while her pulses began to race. Standing there under the gloriously blue sky with his arm about her in that unique spot she felt she could deny him nothing.

'Look at it!' He jerked his head towards the panorama spread below them. 'Isn't it beautiful? Surely you could be happy here.'

'I ... I think so, but ...' she hesitated. 'Would we have to live with your mother?'

For that was a very big fly in her honey.

'No,' he said, to her relief. 'I've been urging her for years to get rid of that house and go into a flat. I expect she will now she'll be alone. The house is obviously much too big for her.'

He went on to say that he thought they also should have a flat, a modern one with a large balcony on which they could display potted plants. They would go and look at some and of course she should furnish it just as she chose.

'You're very generous, Damon,' she told him gratefully.

'I want to make you happy. For the present, please try

to bear with Hermione. She has old-fashioned ideas and she's outspoken, I know. It's always hard for ageing people to keep up with modern trends, they move so fast, but as soon as we're married,' his arm tightened, 'you won't see very much of her. She has her own interests that keep her busy.'

Violet shadows were creeping down over the mountains, a little breeze from the sea stirred the golden air. Audrey drew a deep breath, and through the close clasp of Damon's arm some of his impatience was communicated to her. Why wait to let the outside world, relatives and friends impinge upon their happiness? Why bother with doubts and questionings? Seize what was offered to her and make sure of it, then she and Damon could find fulfilment together.

'As soon as we've found somewhere to live ...' she began shyly.

'That won't take long. I've influential connections,' he told her.

'Then ...' She let the word hang between them.

'You mean you'll marry me without going back to England?' His voice was as eager as a boy's. 'As soon as it can be arranged?'

'Yes.' She buried her face in his shoulder.

'Excellent,' he said with satisfaction. Regardless of possible onlookers, he raised her face and kissed her passionately on the lips.

CHAPTER SEVEN

AUDREY returned from the Acropolis in a state of ecstasy, and content to allow Damon to direct her destiny. He had completely dispelled her slight despondency, and her heart and mind were submerged in dreams of their rapturous future together under the same roof, which was to begin in so short a time.

During the evening he put a call through for her to her home. Her father answered the phone, but the line was bad and the time limited. She merely said she was staying on in Athens to see more of the city as Mrs Grivas' guest, information which did not seem to surprise him.

'Don't do anything rash,' he counselled her, 'but what about your job?'

'Oh, I'll let them know,' she said vaguely, and promptly forgot all about it.

Damon wanted a very quiet wedding to take place as soon as the formalities were completed, probably in a fortnight's time, and with that she concurred. She knew that her mother would be disappointed to be defrauded of all the trimmings attendant upon her only daughter's marriage, but she shrank from the fuss, bother and delay which a return to England would entail. Her association with Damon had a dreamlike quality and it was fitting it should culminate here in this fabulous city after her enchanted cruise. Also she gave heed to Hermione's warning: 'Procrastinate and you'll lose him.' Not that she really accepted that possibility, it was a slur upon Damon, but her instinct was to make sure of her happiness without delay.

Damon told her his father would find the necessary

flat; he owned property in the city, and he opened an account for Audrey at a multiple store to buy what she thought necessary in the way of linen.

'Mama will expect you to provide that,' he told her with a quizzical look. 'Greek girls start collecting it from an early age.'

She had some money of her own left over from her holiday to purchase such fripperies as appealed to her. Clothes she had in abundance from her cruise outfit until the weather turned colder—by then she would be Damon's wife. Actually she gave very little thought to practical matters, her whole being was absorbed in her lover; Damon had become her world.

Hermione became almost affable, approving Damon's plans, but she insisted that he must find other accommodation. It was not seemly, she declared, that bride and groom-to-be should live under the same roof, and to Audrey's disgust he gave in to her and went into lodgings. Actually this made little difference to her, for he went to work early in the morning but came to the House of the Olives directly after siesta time—the hours between two and four when everything shut up—to take her out, a proceeding his mother deplored but upon which he insisted. Audrey occupied her mornings with shopping and sightseeing.

She had been three days in Athens when Matthew Gregory arrived. Damon and Audrey, returning from dinner at a restaurant, found him ensconced in Hermione's salon as if he were still master there, though actually he had booked in at the Hilton.

'Well, my boy, you've done it at last,' he said heartily, after they had greeted him, Audrey with reserve, for she was not at all pleased to see him. Intuitively she felt that his coming presaged trouble. 'I arranged to fly out as soon as I received your radiogram. She'll make you a good wife, Damon, I've watched her grow up and there's no permissive nonsense about her.'

'I should hope not,' Damon exclaimed, laughing. 'And if she develops any, I'll beat her.'

'She won't,' Matthew declared confidently. 'Good bourgeois stock and well principled. So, Audrey my child, you're happy?'

'Very,' she smiled at him. 'But you're a devious old man—you engineered it all, didn't you? Sending me on that cruise!'

He laughed and raised her chin with one large hand.

'Stars in your eyes, I see. Boy has to meet girl somewhere, and what more romantic than a ship at sea? I congratulate you, my dear, he's an elusive devil, but I'd high hopes you'd pull it off.' He shot his son a barbed glance.

'I didn't have much chance with the two of you in league against me,' Damon observed ungallantly, and the look that accompanied his remark sent a shiver down Audrey's spine. She sensed he resented his father's attempts to manipulate him, but why should he do so when the outcome had been such a happy one?

Matthew told her that he had informed her father of what was happening, and Arthur had accepted the inevitable, as he put it.

'I'm afraid your mother was a bit reproachful,' he said, 'but I explained that as we'd got you here, we weren't going to let you go.' He gave her a mischievous grin. 'It might be possible to fly them out for the ceremony. We'll see.'

Though they lived separate lives, Matthew was on friendly terms with his wife. Audrey discovered they had a common bond in their business interests, in which Hermione was astute. No one could get the better of Kyria Grivas in a deal.

'Mama could run a shipping line single-handed,' Damon told Audrey. 'I'm glad you've no talents in that direction, it would be like going to bed with a computer.'

He often made unexpected and casual references to their coming intimacy for the pleasure of seeing her blush, and she never disappointed him.

Certainly, except for her son Hermione displayed no warmth of feeling towards anyone, and Audrey feared her initial dislike of herself was due to her lack of dowry, but she seemed to have got over that and treated her with the same cool courtesy that she extended to Matthew. He was staying at the Hilton until after the wedding, and as Damon had said, he found a flat for them, and he spent most of his spare time at the House of the Olives.

Damon had his own car and took Audrey to Sounion, where the remains of the temple dedicated to the sea god Poseidon stand on a barren headland as a landmark for ships at sea, and to Vouliagmeni, which he said would be a change from ruins as it were a seaside holiday centre with sandy beaches and small restaurants.

But he was changing, and although on these excursions he was considerate and courteous, he was always a little aloof and seemed to avoid contact with her, and his goodnight kiss was a mere brushing of her lips. This diminishing ardour worried her, and one evening after returning from a trip to the pine-clad foothills of Mount Hymettus she voiced her anxiety.

'Damon, are you sure you're not regretting this hasty marriage?'

He had come round to open the car door for her and loomed over her, a shadowy shape in the darkness as she made no move to leave her seat.

'My darling, what on earth makes you ask that?'

'You seem to be cooling off,' she said bluntly.

'Cooling off!' The deep note that always stirred her sounded in his voice. With his usual insight he perceived what was troubling her. 'My child, I daren't make love

130

to you,' he said quietly. 'I'm a Greek, not one of your cold countrymen who I think must have ice in their veins. Since you've entrusted yourself to me alone I must behave myself. It wouldn't do to anticipate our marriage.'

This explanation chilled her, for she was hungry for a demonstration of his love, which at times she was beginning to doubt. She knew that Greeks set great store upon virgin brides and he was flouting convention by spending so much time with her alone, and the fact that she had practically asked for the embraces he was not prepared to give caused her to flush with shame, and she was glad of the concealing dark. Surely a kiss now and then could not dangerously inflame him—or could it? For the first time she felt a twinge of fear. What dark volcanic passions lay concealed beneath his suave exterior that so soon would be unleashed upon her?

She said faintly: 'I'm sorry, Damon, I didn't understand.'

'I'm not sure you do now, you're such a child still,' he remarked, thereby infuriating her. Did he imagine she didn't know the facts of life? She got out of the car with immense dignity and said frostily:

'Even children have warm blood and expect caresses.'

He laughed delightedly. 'That sounds promising. You only have to be patient a little longer, darling.'

He left her to enter the house while he put the car away, and she went reluctantly up the steps. Ever since the night in Istanbul she had had a feeling of unreality. She could hardly believe that she was in fact about to marry his dark magnetic stranger and live with him in the flat with the flower-filled balcony that Matthew had found for them. Would she wake up one morning and find it had all been a dream?

A week before their wedding day, Damon had to go to Spain in connection with the conversion of a cruise liner. He would be away two nights. Matthew said he could have gone, but that particular vessel was Damon's pigeon and he was sure he would want to see to it himself, and Damon agreed that he would.

'Will you mind terribly?' he asked Audrey, trying to keep the eagerness out of his face. 'It is rather important, and it's only for two days. I'll be back in plenty of time for the wedding.'

'Of course I mind,' she returned, 'but I wouldn't want you not to go. You must always put your work first.' But her heart sank at the prospect of being left with two people who were not very congenial to her.

'That's the right spirit,' Matthew nodded approval. 'Don't worry, Damon, we'll look after her.'

But she threw away restraint and clung to him when he said goodbye on the night before he was due to leave in the early hours of the morning as if she feared she would not see him again.

They were alone in Hermione's sitting room, Matthew having tactfully removed his wife, who was always loath to leave the lovers alone together, not considering it was proper.

Then Damon did kiss her, close and hard, and finally put her from him with unsteady hands.

'Darling, it's only for two days.'

'I know, I know, but ...'

She could not explain the sense of foreboding that was oppressing her.

'But ...' he chided her. 'But what? Don't be silly, Audrey, I'm not going to the North Pole.'

'Yes, I am being silly. Don't take any notice of me. Soon we'll be together always.' But even then he would have to make business trips, but perhaps he would take her with him.

'God keep you, my darling,' he said fervently, and was gone.

Next morning Audrey woke with a flat feeling, for

132

there would be no Damon arriving after siesta time. She spent the morning exploring the ruined theatre of Dionysus across the way. She had lunch alone with Hermione, who discoursed upon Damon's likes and dislikes, a favourite theme. After the meal, her hostess retired to her bedroom, but Audrey found the house too hot and stuffy, and she went out into the strip of garden behind it where there was a little arbour at one end covered by a vine which was trained overhead. It was enclosed by a marble wall and was quite private. Here it was shady and comparatively cool. She had brought a book, but soon it slid from her lap and she gave herself up to dreams.

After a while she became aware of voices, Hermione's and Matthew's. Though officially staying at a hotel he was a daily visitor at the House of the Olives. They had come out on to the verandah and were conversing in English, probably in case the servants could overhear. Audrey did not want to make her presence known; it would mean she would have to make polite conversation for which she was disinclined. They were discussing business and she need not listen, nor could she hear all that was said. She wondered what Damon was doing—they had siestas in Spain, didn't they—and if he were resting would he be thinking of her? Then a name caught her attention and caused her to strain her ears.

'Mrs Remington-Smythe has been staying at the Hilton,' Matthew was saying.

'How dare she!' Hermione exploded. 'To show herself in Athens now. Has she no shame?'

'We can't hope that that affair is over,' Matthew said dejectedly, 'but at least Damon's marriage will kill the gossip for the time being.'

Hermione assured him, 'We can but pray they will be more discreet in future. It's a good thing our little English simpleton is unaware of the connection.'

'Of that I am not sure.' Matthew sounded worried. 'The woman was on the *Andromeda* too, you know. I hadn't expected that. Why doesn't her husband come home and look after her?'

'Do you believe that he exists? I am inclined to think he is a myth.'

'Of course he exists, or Damon would have married her, though I warned him I wouldn't countenance a divorced woman. I imagine she's clinging on to her husband until she's seen which way the cat's going to jump.'

'Damon would never be so unfilial as to go against your wishes.'

'Oh, wouldn't he! But he'll think twice before risking disinheritance; he has extravagant tastes, as we both know.' He moved uncomfortably and the wicker chair in which he was sitting creaked. 'Damn it all, Audrey's a sweet child. What more can he want?'

'Unfortunately she is still a child and she wearies him,' Hermione said in her cold penetrating voice. 'She allows her feelings to show too plainly. That one has not the art to hold a man. You should have married him to a Greek.'

'No good Athenian family would accept him after the talk about Mrs Remington-Smythe,' Matthew growled. 'Luckily the Winters won't have heard it. I thought the substantial dowry I'm giving Audrey would have ensured his good behaviour, but I suspect he's taken her to Spain. I ascertained that she checked out of the Hilton this morning early.'

'If Audrey should give him a son he may reform,' Hermione suggested hopefully.

'Possibly, and I'll make their son my heir. I'm certainly not going to leave my money for him to squander on Mrs R.-S.' Matthew declared. 'She's flaunting a diamond pendant which I suspect he bought for her. It's my fortune she's got her eye on, the harpy, and she'll not let him go while she's a hope of getting some of it.' He relapsed into gloomy silence, which was broken by the shrilling of the telephone inside the house. 'Ah, that'll be my call to London.'

The wicker chair creaked again as he got to his feet. Whether Hermione followed him Audrey neither knew nor cared. She sat on as still as a marble statue until dusk fell. Her golden dream had dissolved like mist before the harsh wind of cruel reality, and she had been brought crashing down to earth.

The conversation she had overheard had indicated with devastating clarity that Damon's advances towards herself had been all pretence. He needed a cover for his liaison with Daphne and at the same time he wanted to keep his father sweet because he did not want to jeopardise his inheritance. Matthew had bribed him to marry her, by giving her a dowry that she did not want and the bestowal of which humiliated her. A practised lover, Damon had set out to win her with his tongue in his cheek and had succeeded only too well. Cruellest cut of all, Hermione had said she wearied him.

Her instinct had been true when she had been distressed by his aloofness. He had retreated because Daphne was waiting for him when he had done his duty by herself, and when the Spanish trip was proposed he had jumped at the opportunity to take her away with him. Audrey winced as she remembered how she had clung to him at parting, naïve soft fool that she was to be so easily deceived with sweet words and tender glances. Damon was adept at both, but they meant nothing. Once he had told her that he had outgrown romantic love; good-looking girls were to him a diversion and a means to assuage an urge. He had only agreed to marry her because it had been made worth his while to do so.

Extravagant tastes! His big car, his stylish clothes, his lavish spending, at what sum had Matthew valued her to tempt him? Mrs Grivas had accepted her as a means to silence scandalous tongues; the reprobate was marrying a young bride, so he must be going to settle down, the gossips would say, but would he? Daphne would still be there. Even when he had bought her engagement ring he had gone back to procure that much more valuable pendant to placate his mistress, and Daphne, secure in the knowledge that her hold over him had not weakened, had countenanced the betrothal as a necessary evil and had looked at her with pity.

Cheryl had warned her that she had not seen the last of Mrs Remington-Smythe, and Cheryl had the right attitude towards Damon; he was not to be trusted an inch, while she had been blindly besotted as she had told her.

Darkness had fallen over the city, pierced by its myriad lights. The floodlit Acropolis shone above the house, a golden wonder. Caught by its spell, she had weakly given into Damon's wish for a speedy marriage, a wedding that was to take place a week hence—only now it would never take place.

What was she going to do? Confess to her eavesdropping and denounce him? Hermione and Matthew would take his part, they would seek to convince her that she had misheard or misunderstood. While as for Damon ... she closed her eyes and shuddered. In spite of her despair and disillusionment she feared she might succumb if he resorted to physical persuasion. Her body yearned for his touch, though her mind revolted from his duplicity.

She would like to leave there and then, but she had very little money left, certainly not enough for her expensive fare home. She could appeal to her father to send her some, but that would mean delay and though the Winters were adequately well off a sudden demand for a large sum might embarrass him. Nor did she fancy being stranded in a strange city. She had got herself into this mess by her own folly and she must get herself out of it without help. Reluctant though she was to see him again, she would have to face Damon and persuade him to send her home. She could say that she had changed her mind about living in Greece, and that was an argument he could not refute.

Meanwhile she had to face dinner with Hermione and her godfather—Matthew dined with them most nights—without allowing them to suspect that she had discovered how they were using her. She squared her shoulders; anger and indignation would carry her through, she would meet guile with guile.

The Audrey Winter who awoke next morning was a changed person from the unsuspecting, ingenuous young girl who had set out so blithely upon her summer cruise. She had grown up. At dinner she had laughed and talked with unusual animation, although her heart was hot and bitter against her two companions; Uncle Matt who had sent her to meet his son because his own countrywomen would not have him, and Hermione who was using her as a stooge while secretly despising her. Little they knew that all their scheming was for nothing and she was going to walk out on them! To be fair, they believed that she would be doing well for herself by this marriage. Damon was comfortably off in his own right apart from his expectations, and they would believe money compensated for heartbreak. They were an unscrupulous, devious pair and she hoped that once she had gone, she would never see them again. She had read somewhere that the Greeks admired cunning, a trait exemplified in one of their ancient heroes, Ulysses.

She deliberately fanned her sense of outrage because she had yet to confront Damon, and that was going to hurt for all her passionate anger. She tormented herself with visions of Damon and Daphne together in Spain, laughing no doubt at her naïveté, believing her lulled into false security by Damon's protestations of love—only now she came to think of it, though lavish with endearments he had never once actually said he loved her. What he had said was that he was incapable of it.

Nor did Audrey deceive herself that he would drop Daphne if he married her. They were too deeply involved and she was the one who would be neglected, perhaps deserted; how could she hope to put up any sort of rivalry to the other women's sophisticated beauty? Throughout the cruise she had felt herself inferior. But that did not excuse Damon; he was a cynical selfish brute incapable of fidelity or even decency, and thank God she had found him out in time!

Intuitively she knew that she would gain nothing by upbraiding him, much as she wanted to do so, for passion on her part would incite passion in him, and that was what she dreaded. She must stick to her assertion that she had had second thoughts about living in a foreign country and with his mother's example before him he would accept that. He had told her she must be sure and as he had tried to rush her he had only himself to blame for her change of mind. She wished it was not necessary to ask him for her fare home, but it was only right that he should pay it, for he had insisted that she should stop off at Athens and forfeit the rest of her cruise ticket.

Her inner turmoil produced a bad headache, and it was with relief that she accepted Hermione's suggestion that she should not come down after her siesta but have dinner quietly in her room and go to bed early with a couple of codeines.

'Pre-bridal nerves,' Audrey heard her say to Matthew, and then to her, 'You must look your best to welcome Damon home tomorrow.'

The welcome he was going to get from her was not what they expected, Audrey thought grimly. Having slept little on the previous night, she did sleep soundly and awoke refreshed and calmly resolute.

It was anticipated that Damon would arrive in time for dinner, which Hermione insisted that he must eat with the family. 'No doubt you wish for him to go out and have him to yourself in that strange foreign fashion of yours,' she said acidly, 'but you are not yet his wife and I am his mother.'

'Of course we'll dine with you, I've no wish to defraud you of his company, madame,' Audrey returned formally, adding mentally; now or ever.

Nevertheless the meal would be something of an ordeal, and as soon as it was over she must get him alone to tell him of her decision. She hoped that on the next morning she would be on her way.

Audrey dressed with care in one of her holiday dresses, the 'green thing' that Damon had said became her. She remembered his remarks about haute couture; he must have been thinking then that she would need some grooming to be presentable as his wife. He had known what he had to do and was nerving himself for the task. She supposed that according to his lights his actions were not as despicable as they seemed to her, because Greeks always favoured marriages of convenience, and until recently they had been the rule and still were among the country people. Men pursued the girls with the biggest dowries and love was not part of the bargain. Only then she had had no idea that her godfather had dowered her to make her acceptable.

She was unusually flushed and her eyes shone with the light of battle as she heard Damon's car draw up at the gate. She went slowly downstairs, giving his mother and Matthew time to greet him before she appeared. Matthew was already questioning his son about the business when she entered the salon, and her heart gave its customary thump as she caught sight of Damon looking so lithe

139

and debonair in his evening clothes. He must have been to his lodgings to change before coming to the house. She knew where he was staying, but she had never been there; Hermione would have considered it most improper that she should do so, but she didn't doubt that Daphne had been a frequent visitor.

Damon broke off his conversation with his father as she came in and came to meet her.

'Have you missed me?' he demanded playfully, as he bent to kiss her cheek, the most he would do with his parents present.

'Of course,' she returned coolly, turning her head away from those treacherous lips that only a short while previously must have caressed another woman, and not on her cheek. 'But you'll have been too busy to miss me.'

'But I did, especially in the evenings.'

'Really? I should have thought you'd have been too well entertained.'

He frowned at her tone. 'It was a business trip,' he reminded her. She opened her eyes very wide.

'But don't they fête their visiting tycoons?'

She was speaking at random, for in every fibre she was conscious of his virile presence beside her—and his deceitfulness, she must not forget that. He had had Daphne with him.

'I don't suppose Damon had any time for relaxation,' Matthew intervened. 'He had to compress a great deal of work into a short time.'

'What hard luck!'

Audrey met Damon's puzzled eyes. She thought, did you have no time to wine and dine her? Of course you did.

Sensing some sort of tension, Hermione said: 'We are all so happy to welcome you back, my son, and to Audrey I am sure the short period has seemed over-long.'

'A century!' Audrey exclaimed with truth. During his

140

absence her universe had toppled.

Damon was not lacking in sensitivity. He watched her covertly throughout dinner with anxious eyes, or was it guilt she read in them? She talked and laughed with brittle gaiety, recounting incidents of the cruise.

'Damon was brilliant at deck games,' she told them, 'but I only shone once, at the fancy dress parade.' She threw Damon a challenging look. 'But he didn't like my costume and tried to stop me getting the prize.'

'It didn't suit her,' he said curtly.

'That wasn't the point, you weren't being fair.' Then before he could retort, 'I suppose Daphne went on to Dubrovnik? She must have missed you, for you were the only person she condescended to be matey with.' Her eyes were wide and innocent, her expression ingenuous. Inwardly she gleefully noted Matthew's and Hermione's uneasy looks, but Damon was unruffled and he said coolly:

'Mrs Remington-Smythe was an excellent bridge player and her interest in me was concentrated upon that game which I also play. That's something I must teach you, Audrey, it's a social asset.'

You lying hypocrite, she thought wrathfully, but she remarked calmly that she didn't care for cards.

When they had eaten their dessert and Audrey had been playing with a peach because she had very little appetite that night, Matthew announced that he could wait no longer to hear the details of Damon's transactions, and if the ladies would excuse them they would like to be left alone to talk business.

'We'll join you later for coffee,' he suggested.

'That will be most late, I think,' Hermione said, smiling. 'I had better send yours in to you.'

'I'm sorry,' Audrey spoke with decision, 'I'm afraid you'll have to restrain your impatience, Uncle Matt, until another occasion. I've something I must say to Damon

141

that is urgent and private, so perhaps you and Mrs Grivas would be so good as to leave us.'

All three looked at her in startled surprise. It was so unusual for Audrey to assert herself. She had risen from her chair, a slim green figure taut as a drawn bow with resolution in the lift of her chin.

'My child, much as we sympathise with your desire to be alone, it is not correct at this late hour,' Hermione objected.

'I'm not a child, I'm an adult,' Audrey returned. 'I'm also British and I don't accept your conventions, madame. After tonight ...' her voice trembled, but she quickly controlled it, '... my behaviour will be a matter of indifference to you.'

A faint alarm showed in the green eyes. 'That is a very strange thing to say ...' she began, and Damon interrupted her.

'Mama, please to leave us, and you too, Matt. I would like to speak to Audrey alone.'

Reluctantly Hermione turned towards the door. Matthew, though uneasy, tried to laugh the tension off.

'My boy, I fancy she suspects you've been ogling the *señoritas*.' Then sternly to her, 'Don't be silly, Audrey. You say you're an adult, behave like one.'

She met his dark eyes with a flash of steel in her grey ones.

'I shall, Uncle Matt. Please go.'

He raised his shaggy brows, but he went. As the door closed on his exit, Damon deliberately poured himself another glass of wine.

'Has someone been telling tales?' he inquired pleasantly.

'Are there tales to tell?' she retorted.

Abruptly she sat down again at the table, resting her elbow on it, her chin in her hand.

'It's nothing like that, Damon. It's simply that I ...

I've been thinking very hard while you were gone, and I've decided I can't live here after all. As I said just now, I'm British, I shall always feel British, and when the novelty of life here has worn off I'll be homesick. Your city is a lovely place, but it's alien.' She could not look at him, her eyes were fixed on the tablecloth. 'You told me I must be sure I could accept your country as my own. Well, I find I can't and I never shall.'

She finished her little recital that was so far from the truth and waited anxiously for his reaction. If only he would accept her reason and then there need be no violent scene, no recriminations, no excuses and denials. Though her heart was hot and sore against him, she did not want to be provoked into angry denunciations. Let them part with dignity.

The silence that followed was so prolonged that at last she ventured to raise her head to look at him. What she saw terrified her. His face was livid, his eyes smouldering, his lips drawn back; he looked like a devil. With a little cry she cowered back into her chair, covering her face with her hands. What was he going to do to her? Kill her?

Minutes passed, and then he said quietly:

'It's a little late, my dear, to change your mind. The flat is rented and furnished and Matthew has been planning to bring your parents out for the ceremony as a surprise for you.'

'Oh, Uncle Matt's planning!' she exclaimed vehemently. 'Must he be always interfering?'

'Is that what has vexed you?'

Looking up, she saw that Damon had regained his self-control. Except that he was paler than usual, he appeared normal.

'No,' she said tonelessly. 'It's true I resent being managed, but it's not that. You promised you wouldn't rush me, but you have. I want to go home.'

In spite of her declaration of adulthood her last sentence was the wail of a lost child. She was snatching at the recollection of her happy uncomplicated childhood, before she had met Damon and been plunged into this emotional whirlpool. A vain aspiration, for she had progressed too far from that serene state to ever recapture it.

Damon said, 'Your home is here.'

'But I've just been explaining,' she cried desperately, 'I can never feel it is.'

'Look at me.'

Unwillingly she raised her eyes to his to meet his probing gaze. Such beautiful eyes he had, that could express so many things and most of them false, she thought bitterly. Fearing what he might read in hers, she turned her head away.

'Will you please arrange for me to go back to England?' she asked unsteadily.

'No.'

The curt monosyllable startled her. She had not expected such an unqualified refusal.

'Then I'll have to appeal to the British Consul to help me,' she said defiantly, for that possibility had occurred to her.

'You'll do no such thing.'

'But, Damon, you can't keep me here against my will.'

'Can't I?'

He was trying to frighten her, she thought feverishly, but she would not let him intimidate her.

'No, of course you can't,' she said crossly. Then she played her trump card. 'Do you want our marriage to be like your father's? Me in England, you here?'

'I'm sure our marriage won't be in the least like Matthew's and Hermione's,' he told her suavely. 'Because though I may be like my dear papa, in some ways you bear no resemblance whatever to my respected

144

mama. To start with, theirs was a union of two communal enterprises; Hermione's people are also in shipping. It was arranged.'

'And isn't ours?'

'Certainly not. Papa Matthew may have engineered our meeting, but he's had nothing to do with the outcome.'

'Only to tempt you with a dowry that I knew nothing about, and would refuse to accept if I could.'

'It is I who does the accepting. Is that what has upset you? Hermione perhaps told you? From her point of view she may have thought you might feel ashamed to come to me empty-handed. He is only advancing some of the money that will come to me eventually, so that we can set up housekeeping in style. It's often done. Saves income tax.'

Audrey frowned. She had been led into betraying more than she had meant to do. The dowry, much as it irked her, was not the real grievance. She reverted to her former argument.

'That's only secondary, it's not important, though I'm sorry you couldn't accept me without monetary compensation,' she said bitterly. 'No,' as he started to speak, 'let's return to the real issue. I meant what I said. I don't want to live in Athens.'

'Would you be content to live somewhere else?'

She was silent, staring at him, she had not expected such a concession. He came round to her side of the table, pulled out a chair and sat down beside her.

'Suppose you drop these prevarications and tell me truthfully why you want to jilt me?'

It was no use, she would have to tell him since it was the only way to make him free her. 'Daphne,' she said, and the mere mention of that hated name broke her brittle calm bringing a resurgence of her bitterness and scorn.

Damon sprang to his feet and walked away from her. Standing with his back to her, staring at the curtained window, he asked:

'What about her?'

'What ... oh really, Damon, isn't she your mistress? Weren't you making love to her while you were trying to make up your mind to propose to me? Didn't she follow you here and put up at the Hilton? Uncle Matt saw her there, so you can't deny it. Aren't you using me as a cover-up for your affair with her? And didn't she go to Spain with you?' Her anger gathered momentum as she recited his misdemeanours. Rising to her feet, she went on passionately, 'You thought I was so simple and child-like that it would be easy to deceive me, but I've found you out. I can't marry such a despicable double-dealer as you've been proved to be. I hate you, I loathe you!'

Her voice rose hysterically and she was near to tears, for she knew that however big a heel he was he still held her heart, and her profession of hate was only a facet of her love.

'Be quiet!' he said sharply. 'Sit down and pull yourself together. You wouldn't like my treatment for hysteria.'

Weakly Audrey subsided into her chair and tried to calm herself. She had said all the things she had meant not to say, she had made her accusations, and he seemed no whit ashamed or even perturbed.

'So you're prepared to judge me on hearsay without giving me a chance to defend myself?'

She ventured to steal a glance at him and saw that though his face was calm his voice controlled, his eyes had the cold glitter of black ice.

'I don't see how you can defend yourself,' she said dully. 'The whole thing is obvious, only I was too dumb to see it ... and I don't want to hear any more lies,' she went on quickly, as he began to speak. 'You've a honey tongue, Damon, I don't doubt you can make black seem white, but you can't explain away this. Why, even in Istanbul ...' she faltered, that had been such a perfect night, but even while she had lived it she had known it was a fantasy, an impossible dream, '... when you bought me a ring ... that ring ...' she pulled it off and laid it on the table. 'You went back to get that gorgeous star for her ... in case she felt neglected, I suppose. I saw her wearing it, and even then I didn't put two and two together.'

'I had a reason ...'

'Oh, no, no ... haven't I said I can't believe anything you say? Let's leave it at that.' A great weariness crept over her, it was all so sordid. 'I ... I don't enjoy abusing you, Damon, but I can't ...' she bit her lips to still their trembling '... share you with another woman.'

There was a pregnant pause, and dumbly she sensed that she had struck home. If only he would declare that Daphne was nothing to him; but she knew that would be untrue and he knew she would not believe him. When finally he did speak his voice was cold and cutting.

'If there's one thing I can't stand it's a jealous, vituperative woman. I thought my wood nymph would be gentle and trusting, but it seems she didn't exist. Well, my dear, we appear to have had a lucky escape. You shall go back to England, I'll arrange it as soon as possible.'

It was over. She had won her release. She rose slowly to her feet, blinking to keep her tears from falling. He was not the only one who had created a being that did not exist.

'Thank you,' she whispered. 'I ... I'll say goodnight.'

Their eyes met, and a sudden flame leaped in his. With a smothered exclamation he swept her into his arms. His embrace was punishingly painful as he crushed her hard against him. His hot lips ravaged her face and throat, and lower to the cleft in her low-necked dress. She was limp

147

in his hold, her pulses throbbing in unwilling response, too overwhelmed to resist. He lifted his head, looked down at her white face, closed eyes and slack mouth, and laughed brutally.

'I could take you now and you would welcome me in spite of all your nasty accusations. Were I the cad you accuse me of being, I would, but though you may not believe it I'm no seducer of innocence. Nor will I permit myself to be insulted by a silly little girl who doesn't know what she's talking about. Go home and find some stupid milksop who has no more idea of how to live than you have, and much joy may he give you! *Adio.*'

He flung her away from him with an almost savage movement, and she caught at a chair to save herself from falling. Without a backward look, he strode out of the room. Audrey heard him go into the salon, Matthew's aggrieved voice and then the closing of the door. Bruised, shaken, she crept upstairs to her room, thankful that there she could weep without restraint.

CHAPTER EIGHT

IT was two days before Damon could obtain a seat on a flight home for Audrey and she had perforce to spend the time at the House of the Olives. Neither Hermione nor Matthew said anything to her about her break with Damon, and she divined that he had forbidden them to do so, nor did he come again to the house while she was there. When she met her hostess at meals, conversation was about impersonal matters, but she saw reproach in Matthew's eyes. He would be returning to London too, but he was allowing her to go first, thereby indicating that he had no wish to travel with her. Subtly he made her feel in disgrace, though the fault was not hers.

She rang up her parents, briefly telling them that she was coming home and the wedding was off. There was no time for lengthy explanations, for those they would have to wait. She insisted that she must pay for the call, being loath to be under any further obligation to Hermione, and Mrs Grivas shrugged her shoulders and accepted the correct number of drachmae from Audrey's scanty resources. Damon was paying for her flight ticket, but that she considered only fair.

Her ring had been found by a servant and brought to her room, but that Hermione refused to touch.

'You should return it to my son.'

'But I shan't be seeing him again.'

Mrs Grivas gave her a black look. 'You are unreconcilable?'

'It's final, yes, and aren't you pleased, madame? You never thought I was a suitable choice for your son.' Audrey winced inwardly as she spoke. Had there ever

149

been any question of choice on Damon's part? He had
regarded her as a convenient dupe to be wooed and won
for his own purposes, and that she had attracted him
physically had been an unexpected bonus. Superficially
he was susceptible, but no woman, least of all herself,
could combat his long devotion to Daphne.

'You were ... adequate,' Hermione conceded coldly.
'Now I doubt that he will ever take a wife.'

Not unless Daphne became free.

'But please to keep the ring,' she went on. 'He would
only give it to ... someone, who has had far too much
from him already. But please not to leave it about on
tables,' she concluded sharply. 'It gives temptation to
my servants.'

Audrey put it in her handbag, thinking that she could
give it to Matthew at some future date.

She spent her last afternoon on the Acropolis, for she
knew her father would ask for descriptions of it. The
small Temple of Athena Niké was almost completely
restored, a gem of Ionic architecture, and she lingered
there for some time, her surface mind absorbing its details. She identified the rock from which Aegeus was
supposed to have hurled himself to death when he saw
his son's black sail and believed he had perished, thus
naming the sea that had been called after him. He must
have had good eyesight, Audrey reflected, for the sea was
a long way off, or perhaps it had been nearer in those
far-off days. The heartbroken old man had taken the
easiest way out, but such dramatics were not for her; she
must go on living though all the joy and happiness had
gone from her life. It had been short-lived, a brief flower-
ing that had withered and died. She might find someone
compatible in the years ahead to relieve her loneliness,
but there would never be anyone to compare with Damon
in outward seeming. Like the gods of Olympus had so
often done, he had stooped to court a humble maid and

he had proved to be as promiscuous as they had been, beautiful, irresistible and dissolute.

She descended from her lofty pinnacle when it began to grow dark and the place would be closed for the night, leaving her poor little dreams among the ancient marble blocks.

Her mother and father refrained from questioning Audrey when, tired and dispirited, she reached her home. They had been alarmed by the haste with which she had decided to marry and to a man she had only just met, though Uncle Matt had tried to reassure them. True, he had more than once remarked to Arthur that a union between their offspring would be a seal upon their long friendship, but Mr Winter had not taken him very seriously even though he had hinted that he would endow his goddaughter with a settlement in such an event. The failure of Matthew's own marriage and the son's being brought up in Greece had not been recommendations. Arthur would prefer that his daughter formed a less exotic connection with one of her own countrymen, whom he had had a chance to meet before the ceremony. Now it was obvious that something had gone badly awry and he assumed that Damon had proved to be too Greek.

'No doubt Audrey will tell us all about it in her own time,' he told his wife. 'At the moment she needs petting and reassurance.' Which they proceeded to give her.

Audrey remembered guiltily that she had omitted to tell her employers that she would not be returning, and as she had overstayed her leave without explanation she assumed she would have forfeited her job, and also a reference. But she had reckoned without Cheryl's resourcefulness. Her friend called the day after her return seeking news of her, and did not seem surprised to find her home.

'So you're back,' she observed, when Audrey had taken her into her bedroom. 'I thought you would be soon.

Found his proposition wasn't quite what you expected?'

Audrey turned away, unwilling to relate the full story, and Cheryl looked commiseratingly at her drooping shoulders.

'Don't worry, love, I won't ask for the squalid details,' she went on kindly. 'Which I'm sure you want to forget. I'm pleased to tell you I've kept your job open for you in case you needed it.'

Audrey spun round, astonished. 'How on earth did you do that?'

Cheryl must have been very certain she would return. She ought to have written to her, but that also she had let slide during those days of rapture.

'Oh, I spun them a yarn about how you missed the boat at Piraeus, lost your passport and were detained by the authorities,' Cheryl said airily. 'We're slack at the moment, so they weren't in any hurry to replace you. In fact they were quite perturbed about you.' She surveyed Audrey's pale face. 'You look as though you've been kept in solitary confinement, which will support my yarn. I'll tell old sourpuss,' for thus she described the head of the typists' pool, 'you'll be in on Monday and she's not to question you. You've had a rough time.'

Just how rough, Cheryl was not to know. Audrey did not approve of her inventions, though she admired her imaginative powers, but she was relieved she would not have to search for work and could slip back into her old groove as if nothing had happened.

'You're a real pal, Cheryl,' she said gratefully. 'Whatever should I do without you?'

'Take my advice next time,' Cheryl suggested. 'Men!' she snapped her fingers contemptuously. 'Rotters all, but life would be very dull without them. You'll have to learn to cope, and this little experience won't have done you any harm. You used to look younger than your years, but now you look older.'

'I am older,' Audrey told her, 'and much, much wiser.'

Her life resumed its normal course, and since Damon was only connected with that enchanted voyage, there was nothing in her daily round to remind her of him. Both he and her holiday became a memory of 'a many-splendoured thing', and inevitably began to fade as autumn turned to winter. Her parents tactfully refrained from referring to it, and she was careful to avoid Matthew Gregory when he came to see her father. Luckily he did not come often and his visits were usually expected, so she could absent herself when he was due to call.

When Audrey had been back a few weeks, she had her hair cut short and waved. Her shorn locks strewing the hairdresser's floor seemed symbolic of the shedding of her naïve girlhood. The new Audrey, she vowed, would be poised and sophisticated, impervious to masculine wiles. In answer to her father's regret for her flowing hair, she pointed out that the new style was more practical and suited to her age, and he was forced to admit it was becoming. She refused to mope and went with Cheryl to various social gatherings—dancing and discothèques—wishing she did not find them so empty and frivolous, and the young men who sought to date her so uninteresting. Compared with Damon they were poor specimens.

Then one Saturday morning she had an unexpected encounter. It was a bright frosty morning and she had come up to the West End to window-shop. Standing outside Swan and Edgar's she saw reflected in the window a tall shape standing behind her. With a little incredulous gasp, she turned about to meet the hard blue eyes of Daphne Remington-Smythe.

She was wearing a black fur coat and a fur toque on her fair curls, but her face looked pale and drawn. Recognition was mutual, and Daphne said to her surprise, 'Come and have a coffee with me.'

153

Audrey hesitated. Was Daphne going to tell her that she and Damon were to be married? It was the only motive that occurred to her for the unexpectedly friendly invitation; Daphne wanted to proclaim her triumph. Her pride prompted her to refuse, but although she had avoided Matthew and discouraged any talk about her holiday with her parents, she had a secret longing for news of Damon even if it were unwelcome tidings, and Daphne would have been in touch with him.

'I'd love to,' she said mendaciously.

Daphne took her to an unpretentious café down a side street, a choice that astonished Audrey, who would have expected her to patronise something more fashionable. Selecting a table in a corner, where, as there were few customers they were practically isolated, she gave the order to a bored waitress and proceeded to chat about the weather and the city, which she seemed to know very well. When their coffee was set before them, she fell silent, and Audrey wondered how she could approach the subject of Damon. Daphne said abruptly:

'So you jilted him.'

Audrey stared at her wide-eyed. 'He ... he told you that?'

'He tells me everything.' Daphne studied her companion scornfully. 'You little fool! Didn't you know you'd got yourself a man in a million? He was all yours and you threw him away.'

'I had to,' Audrey stirred her coffee mechanically, 'because he wasn't mine at all. He was yours.'

'Mine?' Daphne laughed bitterly. 'I've got my man, and do you know where he is?'

'How could I?' Audrey returned. 'The only reference I ever heard regarding Mr Remington-Smythe was that he was a myth.'

'And so he is,' Daphne corroborated. 'There never has been a Mr Remington-Smythe. Didn't Damon tell you?'

Audrey shook her head, feeling slightly bewildered. 'He was always very unwilling to speak of you and he never mentioned your husband.'

Daphne gave a long sigh. 'Always so loyal,' she murmured.

'To you perhaps,' Audrey flashed, 'but hardly to me. He couldn't be to both of us.'

'A somewhat involved statement,' Daphne drawled with all her old disdainful manner. 'And you deserve to be left to welter in your own morass of regrets—for of course you're regretting him, that is if you're human and not just a prim little prude upheld by your own self-righteousness ...'

'Please,' Audrey interrupted, flushing, 'that's not fair. You of all people should understand ...'

'Understand what? That you were too stupid to appreciate your good fortune? Damon wanted to marry you, yet you ran out on him. Had you taken leave of your senses?'

Audrey repressed her rising temper with an effort. Her actions might appear incomprehensible to Daphne, who she was sure had wanted to be Damon's wife herself, but if her husband did not exist, why had not she annexed him? She said quietly :

'Damon didn't love me.'

Daphne gave an exclamation of contempt. 'Such schoolgirl nonsense!'

'It may seem so to you,' Audrey returned with spirit, 'but I knew he loved someone else.'

The hard face opposite to her softened and Daphne said gently, 'But we were never lovers. Damon was little more than a lad when I first knew him. I'm nearly forty, you know.' Audrey looked her disbelief and Daphne smiled sadly. 'One can do much to preserve one's looks with care and cosmetics. Young men are often attracted by mature women and his adoration flattered me.'

'You've known him a long time?' Audrey asked wistfully.

'All of ten years. Grant, that's my husband, is very fond of yachting.' Her face contracted. 'God help him,' she whispered, then she went on, 'We used to spend our summer holidays sailing in Greek waters, and Damon used to join us every year—he was keen on sailing too, that's how we got to know him. Sometimes we made our headquarters at Corfu'—Saint Spiridon, Audrey recalled with a pang—'at others on an Aegean island.'

She seemed to have forgotten her listener, and her usually hard eyes were full of soft lights as she recalled summer days under blue skies surrounded by blue water.

'My husband was very fond of Damon,' she went on dreamily. 'With me the boy was what you might call reserved ... at first. Then one lovely summer night when we'd put in at Delos, he confided in me. Grant had gone ashore and we were alone on deck. Damon was recovering from a disastrous affair with an empty-headed piece who had professed to love him, then he discovered that she was playing the field with an eye for the biggest bank balance. I believe he nearly killed her when he found out—Greeks can be violently jealous—and of course he ditched her. But he'd been deeply wounded and the scars are still there. He once said I was the only woman he could trust. Over the years we came as near to friendship as a man and a woman ever can; I don't think he wanted it any other way.'

She paused and drank some of her coffee, her beautiful face softened by her memories, while Audrey assimilated what she had been told. Some unknown girl had been the cause of Damon's cynical attitude, but he had given Daphne unswerving devotion, a bond all the stronger because it had not been physical. Or was Daphne lying? What she had seen of them contradicted her assertion.

156

'I won't pretend there weren't some sticky moments,' Daphne went on with a faint smile, 'but Grant was his friend too and neither of us wanted to betray him. Eventually I knew Damon would have to marry, but I dreaded losing him. When he told me you had been selected for him, I'll admit I was jealous.'

Audrey felt a rush of indignation. Daphne had had his confidence, and to her he had reported the progress of his wooing while she had been kept in ignorance.

'I wasn't selected, as you put it, by my own will,' she declared. 'And why should you disapprove?'

'I thought you were too young for him.'

'Too young, and too old!' Audrey's laugh was brittle. 'But you were alone on the *Andromeda*, where was your husband who isn't called Remington-Smythe? Is he dead?'

Daphne's face changed as she dragged herself back from an idyllic past to a grim present.

'No,' she said. 'Do you recall the Ryley-Shaw case?'

Vaguely Audrey did. The man in question had been prosecuted for fraud. As he had held an important position and had been of some consequence, the papers had been full of the case, so that although she disliked police news some of the details had reached her.

'Yes,' she admitted. Ryley-Shaw ... Remington-Smythe; dimly she began to perceive a tragedy.

'Grant Ryley-Shaw is my husband,' Daphne said harshly, and now she looked her full age. Lines of strain appeared about her mouth. 'I don't suppose you've any idea what it meant to me to be suddenly toppled from a position of influence and respect to find myself the wife of a criminal. Most of my fine friends deserted me, but not Damon. He came to England and supported me through all the dreadful days of the trial. Afterwards I meant to divorce Grant and perhaps . . .' Her voice trailed away.

'But you haven't done it yet?' Audrey asked, for this was the outcome that Matthew had feared, and if Damon truly loved Daphne as it would seem he did, he would put her before the loss of his 'expectations'.

Daphne smiled enigmatically. 'That would be the right end for my story, wouldn't it?' she suggested. 'Young lover's devotion rewarded at last. Oh, I begged him to take me away to some Greek island to forget, I was frantic with shame and anguish, but he wouldn't. The man you scorned persuaded me to do my duty. He knew I'd always loved Grant as I could never love another man.' She finished her coffee and deliberately wiped her mouth with the paper napkin provided.

'There will be no divorce,' she said quietly. 'I shall stick to Grant. Actually I've been to visit him today. I shall wait for him and I know he's patient. We can build a new life together in some distant place. I've money of my own, I haven't suffered that deprivation, but it was Damon who persuaded me that Grant's one hope of rehabilitation was through me. If I deserted him he would sink into apathy and probably further crime.'

Her face shone with a new beauty, that of selflessness, and Audrey was even more bewildered by the metamorphosis. That Daphne, the apparently egotistical socialite, should be proving herself to be a heroine was difficult to take in, and if she had misjudged her, had she also misjudged Damon?

'But the cruise ...' she began doubtfully.

'That was Damon's idea. He insisted that I needed a holiday to take me out of myself. He booked me a cabin on the *Andromeda* on which he was travelling himself so that he could look after me. I had changed my name while keeping the same initials, I had to do that—so many of my things are monogrammed R-S. I know you all thought I was snobbish and stuck up when actually I was afraid of being recognised or of giving myself away

158

by some slip, but he did his best to ensure that I wasn't lonely.'

'I see,' Audrey said dully. Every facet of Daphne's story presented a further instance of Damon's love for her. He had come to her and sustained her in her dark hour, persuaded her to stand by her husband, and cared for her tenderly on board, as Audrey had witnessed. Such devotion for transcended any physical connection and was something that she could never have hoped to rouse in him for herself. 'I think you're very brave,' she went on shyly. 'A . . . a wonderful woman.'

Daphne's eyes gleamed with sudden malice. 'But you'd much prefer to believe I was an adulteress and a deceiver. It must be quite a blow to have your preconceived notions turned topsy-turvy, but I wouldn't have bothered to put you right if I didn't feel you've been unjust to Damon. He doesn't deserve to have his name smirched for my sake, and I bet Ma Grivas and that saturnine father of his represented me as a modern Jezebel and him as my willing victim.'

'They didn't say anything to my face,' Audrey admitted, 'but I overheard . . . they thought you went to Spain with him.'

'To Spain?' Daphne looked bewildered. 'When did he go to Spain?'

'For two days during the week before . . . before our wedding day. Uncle Matt saw you checking out of the Hilton the morning that he left. They . . . I didn't know you were in Greece.'

'Good grief,' Daphne exclaimed. 'What poisonous minds some people have! I did have some important business in Athens and I flew back from Venice, but I never saw Damon. It was better not to meet, since there'd been some gossip about us previously. We were indiscreet enough to dine together in public when Grant had to leave me alone for a few days.' Seeing Audrey's conscious look she smiled wryly. 'I suppose that got relayed to you too, and perhaps you wondered about this.'

She put her hand into the collar of her coat and drew out the diamond pendant. Vividly Audrey recalled the moment when Ahmet had shown it to Damon, the shimmering treasures all about her and Damon beside her, her newly-acquired betrothed, his ring on her finger, in that city of brilliance and mystery upon a magic night. Involuntarily she covered her eyes with her hand. Damon had rejected the jewel and later gone back to buy it—for Daphne.

'He gave it to me as a memento of our long friendship,' Daphne said softly, 'which had to end that night as he had become engaged to you. Please don't grudge it to me, it's the last thing he will give me, and he would have given you many fine jewels.'

'I don't.' Audrey dropped her hand and sighed. No doubt he would have done so to compensate for not being able to give his heart, but what were jewels worth compared with love? She looked wistfully at the lovely face opposite to her. 'I'm not surprised he adores you.'

Daphne smiled wryly. 'From a distance,' she declared, 'and the distance increases every year. He's outgrown his boyish admiration for me. Don't think I didn't want him to marry—he needs a wife and he ought to have children to carry on his name. But I hoped he'd pick someone more mature, more capable of understanding him, for rubbed the wrong way Damon can be ruthless, even cruel ...' Audrey winced perceptibly. 'But I believe the selection was made by his father, in the traditional manner.' Again Audrey winced. 'Actually he was quite taken with you, said you were so young and pliant he could mould you to his liking, and you hadn't any of the brashness that makes modern girls so tiresome. But you couldn't appreciate him, could you, my dear, you were looking for a Sir Galahad without spot or blemish and

160

when you discovered he was only human you threw him over.' The blue eyes were accusing.

This speech, so sweetly reasonable, was so many barbs in Audrey's heart, disclosing as it did how lightly Damon regarded her. He had been 'taken with her' and thought he could teach her to fit her position, but he had no strong feeling about her at all. The wild passion of his youth he had expended upon a worthless woman, then for years he had adored Daphne, but Audrey he had merely accepted, thanking heaven she was no worse, because he needed a wife ... words he had used himself when he proposed, and his father had sponsored her. Had she married him he might have become fond of her in time, but more probably he would become wholly indifferent when he discovered her limitations, for she had neither Daphne's beauty nor her poise, and he had been intimate with her for a long time, though Audrey no longer believed that she had been his mistress.

He had tried to explain their relationship when she had accused him, but she had refused to listen to him. If he had really wanted to retain her, he should have made her listen, instead of which he had embraced her brutally to prove his power over her, and then cast her aside, telling her to go and find a mate nearer her own dimensions. She looked sadly at her companion, her eyes betraying the hunger of her heart.

'Have you seen him ... since?'

'Several times. He soon found consolation for your loss, but not women he could marry. I don't think he'll ever marry now.' Again the blue eyes were accusing.

Exactly what Hermione had said. Audrey pulled herself together with an effort; repinings were no good, nor was she entirely to blame for what had occurred.

'It's all very well to put all the blame on me,' she defended herself, 'appearances were against him, and I hadn't understood I was being pushed on to him. He ... he had no love for me, in fact Mrs Grivas said ... in my hearing, that I wearied him.'

'You shouldn't believe all that old cow says,' Daphne remarked calmly. 'Depend upon it, she had her own axe to grind. I'm afraid you're too sentimental, my dear, in which case you might have ended by boring him.'

The waitress brought their check and Daphne rose from her seat. For a moment she stared down at Audrey with a pity that belied her contemptuous words.

'There is nothing we regret more than our lost opportunities.'

It flashed into Audrey's mind that one had presented itself now, and she must not lose it. Springing to her feet, she said breathlessly:

'Daphne, if you see him again ... could you ... would you, tell him I've learned the truth, and I'm so sorry ...' She faltered meeting Daphne's cold stare. 'Do you think he could ever forgive me?'

'I don't know that you'd do yourself much good by grovelling,' Daphne observed judicially. 'The hurt was that you could so misjudge him in the first place. However, should the chance occur I'll put in a good word for you. But don't be optimistic. He's obliterated your memory with the aid of several ladies who, as he told me, are at least honest in that they don't pretend they want anything except money and a good time.'

'Just to know he'd forgiven me would be enough,' Audrey pleaded. A lie, for she knew she wanted much more, but a message would establish contact ,and he might, he just might, reply to it.

He did not, of course, but she had no means of knowing if Daphne had seen him and spoken about her. Instead of avoiding Matthew Gregory's visits she now endeavoured to be present whenever he came to the house, and willed him to mention Damon. He never did.

Desperate, she inquired about his wife. Hermione was very well, he told her, and she had at last been persuaded to leave the House of the Olives.

'Too big and lonely for her now Damon is never home.'

'Oh?' she tried to speak with indifference. 'Has he given up the business, then?'

'Temporarily, but he'll return to it when he's exorcised his restlessness.' Matthew's dark eyes were as accusing as Daphne's had been and Audrey knew he blamed her for his son's defection. 'He's been travelling all over the globe.'

'He's lucky to be able to,' she retorted, wondering if Damon went alone.

'Experience of foreign places is always useful,' Matthew said with finality, and addressed himself to Arthur.

So Damon might be anywhere in the world and was unlikely to have met Daphne, who had decided to live in London so that she could visit her husband, but that Audrey did not know.

She did not return her ring to Matthew as she had originally intended. She wore it on a chain about her neck concealed by her clothes. When she was alone in her room at night she would finger it, recalling every moment of that enthralling night in Istanbul. She knew she was being ridiculously sentimental, as Daphne had said, and she had no right to keep the ring, but that and her memories were all she had left of the man whom Daphne declared she had thrown away, and she had been so right. What did it matter that he had not loved her as she wanted to be loved? Love might have come, miracles did sometimes happen, and at least she would have been by his side. Even if he had been the reprobate she believed, she would have done better to swallow her pride and stick to him, at least she had the advantage of Daphne in years if nothing else.

I'll be one of those old maids, she thought wryly, who cherish illusions of what might have been to the end of their days, but I'll never love a lesser man. Though that might prove to be another illusion too, for inevitably Damon's image would fade and might be replaced by another. But that thought was painful, that she could and would forget Damon.

There was an influenza epidemic after Christmas that year. First Audrey succumbed and when she had barely recovered, both her parents went down with it, and she had to stay at home to look after them while still weak herself. Suffering as she was from post-'flu depression, her life never seemed more bleak. Matthew Gregory became another victim. His secretary gave them the information and said he was very ill. Arthur became worried when there was no further news, and asked Audrey to go and inquire about him.

'I can't go myself,' he was only just up and not fit to go out, 'but you're in circulation again, and you've had the bug. I'm anxious about the old boy, he lives alone and mayn't be properly cared for.'

Audrey was very reluctant to go, but after all Matthew was her godfather and had been generous to her. 'He's sure to have the best of attention,' she declared. 'He can afford nurses ... anything.'

'But when one is sick one wants one's friends,' Arthur insisted. 'Hired help isn't the same thing. Take him some flowers or fruit and a couple of paperbacks. I know he's got everything, but he'll appreciate the attention. Poor old Matt's got no family except an estranged wife and a son on the other side of the world; he's no intimates except us.'

So to please her father Audrey went, reflecting that it was unlikely that she would have to see Matthew. She would present her offerings to whoever was there, with appropriate messages and the news that Arthur also was laid up or he would have come. That should satisfy her father.

It was a raw January day with a grey blanket of cloud lying over the city, and occasional flurries of snow. Audrey's tweed coat had a fur collar which she pulled up over her chin. She wore a woollen knitted cap, fur-lined bootees, and trousers and a thick sweater beneath her coat, but even so she was cold.

Matthew lived in a service flat in Mayfair; Audrey had never been to it before, as he preferred to do his entertaining outside. She had upon occasion been invited to formal meals in restaurants with her parents, meals which she never enjoyed under his critical eye, but most of his contacts with her family were in her home. Arthur had given her full directions and she found the place without difficulty.

There was a porter in the imposing entrance hall who glanced superciliously at her clothes, which were more utilitarian than smart. Only the tip of her nose and her eyes were discernible between cap and collar, and the former she felt sure was reddened by the cold. She carried a bunch of daffodils, first hint of spring flown in from a warmer clime and hideously expensive. Of fruit she had decided Matthew probably had an abundance. A couple of paperback thrillers which she hoped he had not read, reposed in her large handbag; small offerings to a near-millionaire but tokens of good will.

The man asked who she wanted, and when she gave Matthew's name, told her the number of the flat and indicated the lift.

'Top floor,' he said laconically.

Audrey thought of giving him the books and flowers with a message of condolence, but decided such an action would be cowardly. Moreover, Arthur would expect a report upon Matthew's state of health which she could only obtain from whoever was looking after him. Reluctantly she stepped into the lift and pushed the right button. Just what she had against her godfather she was not sure, but he had never shown her any genuine affection and she felt that in his eyes she was merely a pawn to be used, and she knew she had disappointed him by refusing to play his game. His half-blood inclined to the Greek side of him and showed in a belief that women's place was a secondary one, except in the case of his wife. Hermione had been too much for him.

The lift stopped and Audrey stepped out into a wide, carpeted corridor, and went along it looking for the number she required. The whole place was centrally heated and breathed luxury. Her bunch of daffodils seemed totally inadequate, orchids would have been more suited to her surroundings, but they were beyond Arthur's purse.

The corridor was very quiet and deserted—difficult to credit that a sick man was behind one of its walls. Perhaps Matthew had been taken to hospital and her ring would produce no response. Finding the number she pressed the bell, wondering who would answer it; a nurse, a servant or no one at all? It seemed that the last was what would occur, for she waited some moments without an answer. As she was about to ring again, the door suddenly swung open disclosing a small vestibule, and a curt voice demanded:

'What do you want?'

Audrey's knees gave way and the daffodils dropped from her nerveless fingers. The man standing before her was Damon.

Audrey had several times wondered how she would greet Damon if they accidentally met, or more practically how he would react to her. She had never anticipated that she would literally fall at his feet. It was a cold day, she had been weakened by her bout of 'flu and the shock of his unexpected appearance when she had been led to believe he was far away overwhelmed her. She passed right out. She was aware that she was being lifted, and her surface mind being occupied by her mission, she murmured faintly, 'My poor flowers!'

'Isn't it rather poor Audrey?' said the gently mocking voice she knew so well. 'I've had several highly charged encounters with your charming sex, but I've never caused one of you to faint before.'

'I never faint.' Audrey sat up abruptly and the room swirled round her, so that she sank back on to the cushions supporting her.

'You did this time, miss, good and proper,' another voice told her, this time a feminine one. 'You've had the bug too, haven't you, and you ought not to be out at all in this weather. Drink this, it's hot. I've just had a pot sent up for Mr Grivas.'

'This' was coffee with a dollop of spirit in it. Audrey sipped from the cup held to her lips.

'Damon,' she whispered weakly.

'Don't try to talk,' she was commanded. 'Rest a little and you'll soon be all right.'

Audrey caught a glimpse of starched apron; a nurse, of course, attending upon Matthew. She drank some more of the liquid and felt her strength returning.

'That's better,' the nurse approved. 'Your colour's coming back. Feel you can sit up now?'

Audrey showed she could and took the cup from her nurse's hand. Her coat had been loosened, her cap removed, and her hair she was sure would be tousled. She saw that she was lying on a settee in a richly furnished apartment. Thick-piled carpet covered the floor, velvet curtains hung at the windows, the cushions behind her head were ruched satin. The nurse moved an occasional table up beside her—Turkish carved wood inlaid with the mother-of-pearl which Turks were so fond of using for decoration. The room was in no particular style.

Tottenham Court Road hob-nobbed with antiques, the framed watercolours on the walls were originals by well-known artists, and were all of Greece.

'You must excuse me now,' the nurse apologised, 'I must see to my patient. If he's well enough you can see him for five minutes. He's been very ill, but his temperature's come down at last. Finish your coffee and I'll be back shortly.'

She bustled out through an inner door which apparently led into Matthew's bedroom. She had not mentioned Damon, and Audrey began to wonder if he had actually been there at all. She thought of him so constantly, he might have been a hallucination created by her feverish imagination. She put her hand to her head suspecting that her temperature had risen again, but it felt quite cool. Fine idiot I've made of myself, she thought despondently, coming to inquire about an invalid and collapsing on his doorstep!

She finished the coffee and tentatively stood up; she had come out too soon and her legs felt wobbly. She would ask the nurse to telephone for a taxi, for she did not feel equal to facing Matthew. Picking up her discarded cap, she looked round for a mirror to adjust it on her head. There was one on the wall opposite the bedroom door, a big gilt-surrounded one that did not go with the furniture at all. She fumbled for a comb in her handbag and took out the paperbacks, laying them on the table. She moved in front of the mirror, combing her hair over her face preparatory to parting it.

'So you've had it cut off.'

She started violently, throwing back her head to clear her vision. In the mirror she saw Damon standing behind her. He wore slacks and a polo-necked sweater; he had lost his sunburn and his face was the colour of old ivory, accentuating the blackness of his hair and the depths of his dark eyes.

'I always wanted to,' she said defensively, 'and my parents have agreed at last.' Actually she had not asked their permission. Mechanically she combed her hair into place, noticing how pale she looked; she had used no make-up. Most unattractive, she decided as she set her cap upon her head, while she registered that Damon was really present and he had caught her looking her worst. Not that it mattered, she had long since been superseded. Addressing his reflection in the mirror, she went on:

'Daddy wanted news of Uncle Matt, so I came round to ask about him. He couldn't come himself, he's not allowed out. We've all had 'flu.'

'So that's why you're looking like a walking corpse.'

Audrey winced at this unflattering description. 'I had a fairly bad dose. Have you managed to escape?'

'Germs find me too tough, even 'flu germs; but sit down, girl, you can't go yet.'

'Indeed I must.' She adjusted her coat collar.

'But don't you want to see Matthew?'

'I ... I won't disturb him.'

'He wants to thank you for the flowers. A real breath of spring, he said. Nobody thought to bring him flowers, and he loves them.'

'Then I'm glad I did.' She turned round slowly. 'I'm relieved they weren't harmed, and I'm awfully sorry for being such an idiot as to faint on you. I suppose it's because I've been ill, it isn't a habit of mine.'

She was gabbling, she knew; his direct searching gaze was disconcerting her. She owed him a further apology for all her doubts of him, but she did not know how to introduce the subject.

'Plus the shock of being confronted by my villainous self,' he suggested flippantly. 'You couldn't have looked more flabbergasted if you'd met Old Nick himself. You think I'm a sort of relative of his, don't you?'

There was a hard edge to his voice under the flippancy.

and she knew he was remembering the harsh things she had said to him when they had parted.

'Oh, Damon, don't be so bitter,' she faltered. 'I ... I've been unjust ... I didn't know ...'

'Don't distress yourself, all that's over and done with,' he returned cheerfully. 'I was sent for because Papa Matt was so ill. Had I known you were coming I would have issued a warning.' He moved to the window and with his back to her inquired, 'Have you found my successor yet?'

'Please, Damon ...' Her voice broke.

He whipped round and stared at her. 'Don't tell me you're having regrets!' he exclaimed.

At that moment the nurse appeared in the doorway.

'You can see Mr Grivas now,' she said.

Reluctantly Audrey followed her into the bedroom.

Matthew lay in a brass bedstead supported by a nest of pillows. His features had sharpened with his illness and the resemblance to his son was more marked. He had been freshly washed and shaved, and on the table by his bed amidst an array of medicine bottles was a crystal vase containing the daffodils.

'Audrey my dear, how nice of you to come,' he said faintly, his normally strong voice muted, and she felt ashamed of her reluctance to see him. She gave him her father's messages and regrets that he too was incapacitated.

'I'm glad you liked the flowers,' she finished lamely. 'Seemed a silly thing to bring, but I didn't know what else.'

'You couldn't have pleased me more. You're like a spring flower yourself, Audrey, but the roses have faded in your cheeks.' He paused, gathering strength. 'Damon's here,' he said in a stronger voice. 'Why don't you two make it up?'

'Oh, Uncle Matt, please!' She looked round anxiously

to see if Damon had followed her and overheard, but though the door had been left open, he was not visible.

'It would please me very much,' the sick man said.

She sighed. 'You never give up, do you? But it's no use, Uncle Matt. Damon and I are quite incompatible.' Again she glanced towards the door. Pride forbade seeking a reconciliation unless she was sure Damon wanted it too, but that was improbable.

'Pity,' Matthew murmured, and closed his eyes.

The nurse told Audrey she had stayed long enough, her patient was still weak and tired easily.

Damon was idly leafing through the paperbacks she had brought when she re-entered the room. 'Thrillers,' he commented. 'They'll put Matt's temperature up.'

'Oh, nonsense, they're only fiction, and I don't suppose he'd appreciate a love story.'

'Which are also fiction,' he said. 'Boy meets girl, misunderstandings develop, they're torn asunder and reunited on the last page. Ours ran true to form except for the reunion.'

'It isn't a real love story unless there's love on both sides,' she pointed out, watching him closely.

'How true, that's what was lacking. There can't be love without some degree of trust. You were ready to believe every ill of me.'

'Oh, so it was my love that was lacking, was it?' she exclaimed, nettled by this unfair distribution of blame. 'I ... I've discovered I was misled, but you could have explained.'

'You wouldn't listen, you declared every utterance I made was a lie. Now I never bother to explain or excuse myself. My friends have to take me as they find me. If they don't like what they find ...' He shrugged his shoulders and looked at her quizzically. 'Shall I call a taxi for you?'

'Yes, please,' she whispered.

171

She had hoped they were on the verge of clearing up their misunderstanding, but he did not care if they did or not. He had said it was all over and he meant it. She had wanted to apologise, but he had rebuffed her and there was no point in abasing herself further. She watched him with her heart in her eyes as he went to the telephone and made his call. He was thinner than he had been; his fine Greek profile looked like chiselled marble, and as hard. Daphne had said he had gone a bit wild after she had left him, but his face showed no sign of dissipation. She averted her head as he put the receiver down.

'It'll be outside in about five minutes,' he told her. 'Shall we go downstairs?'

'Thanks, but I can find my way,' she said quickly. She wanted no more talk from him. It amused him to taunt her, but it wasn't kind. He must know that she had loved him whatever he had felt about her. As usual he sensed her thought, for as she went to the door he put his hand on her shoulder and said gently:

'Infatuation, my child, is not love, and after seeing me again, you've discovered yours has died. Isn't that so?'

Grasping the rags of her pride she managed to meet his eyes, and say firmly:

'You're so right, it has.'

Then she fled.

CHAPTER NINE

As a result of the emotional upheaval caused by her meeting with Damon, and going out too soon into the cold, Audrey had a relapse. Fortunately Mrs Winter had sufficiently recovered to be able to look after her, but the Winter household was a fairly groggy trio as January turned into February. Matthew Gregory, who was about again, sent them cases of fruit and wine.

'In return for my daffodils,' he wrote on a card.

For Audrey when she was at her worst came a bunch of red roses, difficult to come by at that season, but it bore no message and she concluded that they were also from Matthew.

'Cast your bread, or in this case daffodils, upon the waters and it'll be returned to you a hundredfold,' Arthur remarked upon receipt of all this bounty.

From Damon came no sign, he had apparently left the country; therefore Audrey was astonished when some two weeks later she returned from her first day back at her office to find him in their living room, doing his best to put her slightly flustered mother at ease.

Although quite unprepared for his advent, she did not upon this occasion faint, but eyes and cheeks flew unmistakable signals before she could regain command of herself and manage to quench them. Damon regarded her flush and the light in her eyes with quizzical amusement, and she knew that she had again betrayed herself.

Her father had not yet come home, and Mrs Winter excused herself, saying she must prepare their meal, to which she somewhat diffidently asked him to stay. He accepted, to Audrey's dismay; she knew their cuisine was not up to his standards. Her mother could, with due warning, cook an appetising dinner, but she had had no time upon this occasion. As if he suspected this, he said:

'Don't please put yourself out for me, Mrs Winter, I'll take pot luck.'

'I'm afraid that's what it will be,' Sarah remarked as she departed. 'I hope you like sausages.'

'Love them,' he declared emphatically to her departing back.

Damon turned his attention to the pale girl. Audrey was standing by the electric fire, warming her cold feet. She did not look at him, but she was conscious of him in every nerve.

He said, 'Are you sure you told me the truth? If your infatuation is dead, it seems to be reviving.'

'Oh, you're impossible!' she exclaimed fretfully, turning away and seating herself in an armchair. 'You know you said yourself that all that is over, why try to dig it up? I was just surprised to see you. Why have you come, Damon?'

'To be thanked for my roses.'

'Oh, were they from you?' She was startled. 'There was no card with them. Well, thank you very much—they were beautiful.'

'Who did you think they were from?' he asked curiously.

'Might have been one of many—I do have a few admirers,' she returned mendaciously.

'Only a few? Where are your Englishmen's eyes?'

A reminder that he was Greek and compliments to pretty women flowed as naturally from him as water from a spring. Audrey had recovered most of her looks and her hair had been freshly shampooed and set before going back to work, and she was glad of that. She supposed Damon was paying a courtesy call to inquire if they had all recovered, in which case there was no need to have

174

accepted her mother's invitation and endure the sausages.

'I didn't know you were still in England,' she observed formally.

'I wouldn't leave without saying goodbye.'

He was studying her hair with the familiar assessing look and she touched her hair provocatively.

'Don't you think having it cut is an improvement?'

'I prefer it long, and I suppose it would grow again?'

'How conservative you are! Yes, it would if I let it, but I've no intention of doing so.'

He moved nearer her and lightly stroked her head with his fingertips. 'It's still soft and silky in spite of the un-natural waves.'

She jerked her head away, as to her relief she heard her father's key in the door. Damon's touch had set all her nerves tingling.

'Oh, there's Daddy. Are you really staying for ... er ... supper?'

'If you've no objection. I have been asked.'

'Why should I object? But it'll be very ... homely.'

'All the better. My dear, I'm not an epicure. I've eaten stale bread and goat's cheese in a shepherd's hut and enjoyed it. It's the company that counts.'

But that was different, it suggested adventure, and the meal of which the Winters partook at six-thirty was that good old British institution, high tea. It suited them, for Audrey and Arthur lunched lightly at midday and required something substantial, and the early hour left them free for their evening engagements. Sarah Winter patronised parochial whist drives and bingo sessions, Arthur often went to his club and Audrey occasionally had dates, usually with girl friends to concerts or parties. She didn't believe that Damon, who normally dined elaborately at a much later hour, could possibly find this entertainment anything but an ordeal to be endured politely, and she wondered why he lingered since all was

175

over between them and he could not find her parents very interesting. Also his presence was embarrassing, for she was sure that her father and mother were speculating upon his motives, wondering if he had come to effect a reconciliation. Mrs Winter had been a little overawed by Damon's elegance, but her husband greeted him heartily, saying he was so glad to have at last met Matthew's son.

'Though I did see you several times when you were a child, but you won't remember that,' he told him.

'Did you?' Audrey was surprised.

Arthur turned to her. 'That was before you were born.' He gazed at the younger man thoughtfully. 'Your mother wished you to be brought up as a Greek, Damon, but you're a quarter English, and had your English grandmother survived we should have seen more of you.'

Matthew's mother was too far back to interest Audrey, to whom Uncle Matt had always seemed an old man, and she was uneasily aware that her father's observations were made to indicate to her that Damon was not wholly a foreigner.

Damon remarked; 'My grandfather set a precedent that I shall probably follow.'

Audrey felt a stab; had he still got Daphne in mind in spite of all that had been said? She might become tired of waiting for her husband's release and seek a divorce, when her present mood of self-sacrifice had evaporated. Her father would naturally assume that he was referring to herself. Sarah created a welcome diversion by calling them to come and eat.

Damon consumed sausages and chips, or French fried as Arthur said with a wink, with apparent relish; then home-made cake, scones, cheese and biscuits. His host did make one substitution, a bottle of wine, to be followed by coffee, and Mrs Winter put her brown tea-pot away with a sigh. She preferred her cup of tea.

176

When they had finished, Damon asked,

'Have I your permission, Mr Winter, to take your daughter out? It's a fine night and we might have a drink somewhere.'

Audrey's heart gave a thump; what was coming? She looked eagerly at their guest, but his bland face betrayed nothing.

'I promise to return her at a respectable hour,' he concluded.

'Audrey makes her own decisions,' Arthur told him.

'Well then, Audrey?' The black eyes met hers, completely unrevealing.

'Thank you very much,' she said demurely. 'I'd love to come. I'll get ready.'

She ran upstairs to repair her make-up, in a turmoil of conjecture and anticipation. Had Damon relented, and was she forgiven? He had said she had lied about the death of her infatuation, and his invitation suggested that he had more to say upon that subject. Yet even while hope soared, prudence warned her not to be too sanguine. Damon liked feminine company, he might only be repaying hospitality; but there was no need for him to have come at all and endure sausages and chips unless he had some purpose.

She put on her best coat, the one with the fur collar, and tied a light scarf over her head and went gaily down to join him.

It was a frosty night, the air keen as a knife-blade, the cloudless sky strewn with stars. Damon made for Hampstead Heath. They would walk a little, he suggested, he liked the view over London from the Heath's heights, and go on to the Spaniards. Audrey didn't care where they went so long as she was with him.

She recalled the historic night in Istanbul when as now there had been starshine and no moon. Cities were always exciting after dark with their myriad lights, but when Damon spoke as he drove up the long slope of Fitzjohn's Avenue his words were disappointing.

'Matt isn't recovering as he should. It's too damp and cold for him here. We're going to spend a few weeks in the Bahamas.'

'That's splendid,' Audrey agreed with false brightness. 'Lucky you to be able to get away into the sunshine.'

'From which I gather you'd like to be coming too?'

'Don't tantalise me,' she sighed. 'You know it isn't possible.'

He was silent for some minutes and they reached the Heath.

'Will it be too cold for you if we get out and walk a little?' he inquired, as he drove along its southern fringe.

'Oh, let's, I won't be cold. Frost invigorates me.'

He parked the car and locked it and they set off for a point from which they could overlook the city. Damon drew her arm through his in the old familiar manner to guide her footsteps and again Istanbul seemed very close, but instead of the Galata Bridge they saw the lights of London spread below them, thousands of glittering points of brilliance like a giant's jewellery shop.

'I've seen Daphne,' he said suddenly.

'Yes?' Her heartbeats quickened. Had Daphne given him her message? Was he prepared to overlook his misjudgment of him?

'I understand she told you about her husband,' he went on.

'She did. It's very sad, isn't it?'

'Justice had to be done,' he declared firmly, 'he got what he deserved and he's lucky she's prepared to wait for him. He's in for five years, but he'll get remission if he's well-behaved. Such a waste, he was a brilliant fellow and not without charm, but like so many others he wanted to get rich quickly, and didn't care how he did it.'

Audrey sighed. She had not come up here to talk about

178

the Remington-Smythes, or to give them their correct name, the Ryley-Shaws.

'You're still in love with her,' she stated sadly.

The muscles in the arm beneath hers contracted.

'Why do you say that?'

'Because it's obvious,' she said wearily. 'It's always been Daphne, hasn't it? She told me you'd been devoted to her for years. Oh, I know now there was nothing wrong between you, and she's so beautiful it's not surprising. You've stuck her up on a pedestal and added a halo now she's proved herself to be a noble self-sacrificing wife. Ordinary girls like me haven't a chance to compete, we shrink into mediocrity before such perfection.'

A tinge of bitterness crept into her voice. His invitation had raised her hopes, but he only wanted to tell her he was going away and talk about Daphne's tragedy, believing she would be sympathetic since she had received the other woman's confidence.

'You're talking nonsense,' he told her.

'I'm speaking the truth.' She withdrew her arm. 'Can we go home now? I'm getting cold.'

For she could not bear any more. This walk had none of the warm intimacy of the one in Istanbul. It was a chilly British night and he was as remote as the stars above them.

'We haven't had our drink, it'll be warmer in the Inn.'

'I ... I don't want one. If you don't mind, I'd rather go back.'

To her horror she felt tears start to her eyes and she quickened her pace to a run, intent upon escaping into the dark before he discovered she was weeping. Blindly she stumbled up a side path, hoping that she could recover her composure before he found her, but she caught her foot on a projecting tree root and fell on her face.

'Audrey, where are you, you little fool?'

Damon struck the flame from his lighter to locate her, and it caught the gleam of her light headscarf. He knelt down beside her, his hands moving over her body.

'Are you hurt?'

She couldn't answer, for the repressed tears were streaming down her cheeks, released by the shock of her fall. He uttered a stifled oath and swung her up into his arms and she buried her face in his shoulder while uncontrollable sobs shook her body.

Damon strode rapidly along the way they had come. Reaching the car, he had perforce to let her slide to her feet while he unlocked it. Opening the rear door, he lifted her on to the seat and switched on the interior light.

'Now, where's the damage?' He crouched on the floor half in, half out of the car, and peered up into her pale tear-stained face. She would have to give him a reason for her distress.

'I ... I twisted my foot,' she faltered.

'Is that all?' Relief sounded in his voice. He pulled off her shoes and probed each instep and slight ankle in turn, and she saw that her tights were laddered. 'Doesn't seem to be any swelling,' he went on. 'What on earth made you dive off into the dark like that?'

'I couldn't bear any more,' she said truthfully.

'More what?' He completed his examination of her feet. 'I can't find anything wrong.' He raised himself and hit his head on the car roof. 'Damn!'

Audrey laughed. 'I'm not hurt at all,' she admitted, adding, 'physically.'

'You little fraud! In that case ...' He switched off the light.

What happened next was like the unleashing of a tempest. Audrey found herself caught in a vice-like grip, while his weight pressed her down on the wide back seat. His mouth found hers and leaping flame enveloped her,

180

mingling with the fire of her own awakened desire. Amid a tangle of legs and arms he tried to push her coat away from her quivering body.

'Damn it all, girl, you've got too many clothes on,' he complained.

She laughed shakily. 'I didn't come prepared for this.'

'You might have known . . .'

His mouth closed hers again. He contrived to get his hands beneath her sweater. The touch of her flesh excited him to greater ardour, and finally she gave a gasp of pain.

'Damon, you're squashing me!'

'Serve you right, you've plagued me long enough.' His groping fingers found the ring between her breasts and abruptly he raised himself. 'What have you got there?'

She tried to push him away.

'A . . . a St Christopher . . .'

'Liar.'

He drew away from her and leaned over to switch on the interior light. Audrey dragged herself upright against the further side of the car, her hands clasped over her breast to guard her treasure. Remorselessly he pulled them away and drew up the chain about her neck, disclosing what she sought to conceal. The brilliance sparkled between his fingers.

'My ring!'

'I . . . I was going to return it . . . but . . . it was difficult. I wore it for safety, in case it was stolen.'

Damon began to laugh. 'Of all the ingenuous excuses!'

He bent forward, his hands behind her head, and unfastened the clasp to slide the ring off its chain.

'Suppose we put it back where it belongs?'

'But . . . but . . .'

'Will you stop parroting that objectionable word? It's always *but*, *but* with you. You know you want me, and if I'd any doubts about that, this proves it.' He pushed

181

the ring under her nose. 'And I want you. Must I give you another physical demonstration to convince you?'

'Oh no,' she said hastily. 'You're just pure dynamite, Damon.'

'And you're the fuse that ignites me, and that being so, I'd better put a barrier between us.'

He got out of the car, closed the door and went round to slide into the driver's seat. Reaching in to the dashboard locker, he took out a box of tissues.

'You'd better clean your face, my love.' He handed a wad across to her. 'And then we'll go back and tell your parents we're going to be married as soon as possible and honeymoon in the Bahamas. We'll have to take Papa along, but he won't get in our way. Then it's Athens, and the flat which is still vacant.'

'You've got it all taped, haven't you?' she said tersely, 'But I haven't agreed.'

'*But* again!' He groaned. 'You contumacious woman, must I ensure that you'll have to marry me?'

Audrey's emotion had subsided and she felt cold and tired. She had come out hoping for exactly what had happened, but she experienced no exultation, no satisfaction. Daphne was still troubling her, and she was remembering that though after meeting her again Damon's passion had flared up, he had forgotten her during the intervening months during which he had not been alone.

'Nothing you could do would make me have to marry you,' she told him, 'that's an old convention we've discarded.' He raised his eyebrows. 'At least in England,' she amended. 'I know we can turn each other on, which is fine from the physical standpoint, but marriage is more than that.' His eyebrows descended in a frown. 'You don't love me, you never have. The only woman you've ever loved is Daphne. You'd do for her what she's doing for her husband, but you'd never do it for me. With me it's out of sight, out of mind. It's not good enough.'

She leaned her head wearily against the side of the car and closed her eyes.

'You're talking a load of rubbish,' Damon said harshly. 'I know I've a high regard for Daphne, she's a fine woman and there are precious few like her around, but that doesn't affect my feeling for you. That's grown on me ever since I saw you by the swimming pool.' His voice softened. 'My water nymph, so fresh and untouched, as I found out when I kissed you on the boat deck. You didn't know you were destined for me and that lent spice to the pursuit, but I captured you in the end, and all would have been well if you hadn't got hold of some distorted gossip. Who was it poisoned you against me, Audrey?'

'No one, I merely overheard Uncle Matt and your mother talking. They said you'd agreed to marry me to cover up your liaison with Daphne, and Uncle Matt was settling money on me to gild the pill.'

Even after the gap of months and Daphne's assurance that there had been no liaison, her voice quivered with indignation as she recalled her hurt.

'I can't help what Papa Matt does with his money,' Damon told her. 'I believe he's settled some on his god-daughter, which you are, whoever you marry, and I thought you understood about Daphne. As we were seen about together people drew wrong conclusions. Audrey, I wouldn't want to marry her even if she were free. She's too perfect, cool and aloof. I want a flesh and blood wife with plenty of human failings, as I have myself.'

'I've got those all right,' Audrey admitted with a grin. 'But you seem to have managed very well without me since I left you. Not exactly pining for me, were you?'

'Why can't people control their tongues!' he exclaimed angrily. 'My love, I was deeply wounded by your readiness to believe ill of me and your refusal to listen to me, so I let you go, but I soon regretted it. I should have locked you up until you were ready to hear reason. I suppose you've been told that I sought consolation. I didn't find it, I'd only contempt for the women who ran after me. When I was sent for to come to Matthew I meant to make enquiries about you, but you met me with a fine act of indifference that took me in. It wasn't until I saw Daphne and she told me she was sure you were fretting for me that I decided something must be done to bring you to your senses.'

'But I didn't say ...' Audrey began, stung to learn that Daphne had been instrumental in sending Damon back to her. She could not wholly stifle her jealousy of the woman Damon so much admired and whatever he said now, she was sure that there had been a time when he would have married her if she had been free.

'Of course you didn't,' he cut in. 'But isn't there such a thing as feminine intuition?'

She began to pleat the edge of her coat with agitated fingers, her resentment ebbing fast. Why was she stalling when she wanted Damon so badly? Once they were married there would be no more separation.

He leaned over the seat back and stayed her restless fingers.

'Come, haven't you put up enough resistance to satisfy your pride?' He picked up her left hand and put the ring back on her finger. 'That was the pledge I gave you in Istanbul and since then you've worn it hidden over your heart. Audrey, Audrey, don't pretend any longer. You know you belong to me, and don't you want to go to the Bahamas?'

'Is that bait?' she asked mischievously. On the verge of surrender, she could no longer resist the clamouring of her heart.

'Of course, and I didn't think you'd be able to resist it. I'd like to kiss you again, though you look far from glamorous with your tear-blotched face, but we're too

184

imflammable. You do like to do things the hard way, don't you, Audrey *mou*? Let's go back and tell your people we're engaged again.'

She capitulated, but why could he not bring himself to say that he loved her? The actual words had never passed his lips, though he must have said them without meaning them to many women. He had once said it was the question every woman asked, but she would never do so. He must make the admission unsolicited, but would he ever do so?

Two years had passed. Audrey lay in the luxurious bed in the flat in Athens, the blinds drawn against the blinding sun. She had just returned from hospital and the dark head cuddled against her breast was that of Damon junior, who had recently entered the world. It had not been an easy birth, she was narrow-hipped for child-bearing, and at one time she had been in actual danger. But that was behind her now. She had returned to her home with a fine healthy boy, the fulfilment of her marriage.

The two years had not been all bliss, two such passionate natures were bound to clash, but after each quarrel reconciliation had been sweet, and she was learning how to manage her domineering husband. Damon could be led but never driven. When he knew there was to be a child he had shown her extreme tenderness and consideration.

Her hair had grown to beneath her shoulder blades and it swung softly against her cheeks. Her eyes were luminous as she gently stroked the baby's head, then they shone with radiance as she heard Damon's step. He came in and gazed down at the pair of them with something akin to worship in his eyes.

'I'm not disturbing you? The doctor said you must rest.'

'You could never disturb me, Damon, and I'm so glad to be home. I only needed you to complete my happiness.'

She held out her free hand to him and he dropped on his knees beside the bed, carrying her fingers to his lips. 'My darling, it was when they told me you might not pull through that I realised how much I loved you.'

'You do love me, Damon?'

He looked up at her with dark eyes alight with feeling.

'More even than our son. Audrey, I love you, I love you.'

'At last,' she murmured.

'What?'

'You've said it, but I had to go down to the gates of death to wring it from you.'

'My darling girl, what are you talking about?'

'That you've never said you loved me until now,' she told him.

'But Audrey *mou*, didn't you take it for granted?'

She laughed. 'And you pretend to know so much about women! No woman ever does take it for granted. But now you have said it, you can keep right on saying it until our lives' end.'